"It's my blood that flows in Thomas's veins, and he'll be legally recognized as mine."

"But—"

"My son is entitled to his natural heritage, and my wealth will be his wealth in time, though as he grows I'll pay for his welfare and his education." His brow furrowed. "You will benefit, too."

In the split second when he had first mentioned marriage, Ashley had harbored the giddy irrational notion that he might next be going to say that he loved her. But it was brutally clear that love did not play a part in his thinking.

"You mean that when we divorce after as short a time as possible, you'll give me a lump sum?" she inquired, her voice frigid.

Dear Reader,

We know from your letters that many of you enjoy traveling to foreign locations—especially from the comfort of your favorite chair. Well, sit back, put your feet up and let Harlequin Presents take you on a yearlong tour of Europe. **Postcards from Europe** will feature a special title every month, set in one of your favorite European countries, written by one of your favorite Harlequin Presents authors. This month, come with us to Portugal and discover the Algarve, an interesting region of the country that is also known as the sun worshiper's paradise.

The Editors

P.S. Don't miss the fascinating facts we've compiled about Portugal. You'll find them at the end of the story.

HARLEQUIN PRESENTS

Postcards from Europe

ELIZABETH OLDFIELD

Sudden Fire

Harlequin Books

TORONTO • NEW YORK • LONDON
AMSTERDAM • PARIS • SYDNEY • HAMBURG
STOCKHOLM • ATHENS • TOKYO • MILAN
MADRID • WARSAW • BUDAPEST • AUCKLAND

ISBN 0-373-11676-4

SUDDEN FIRE

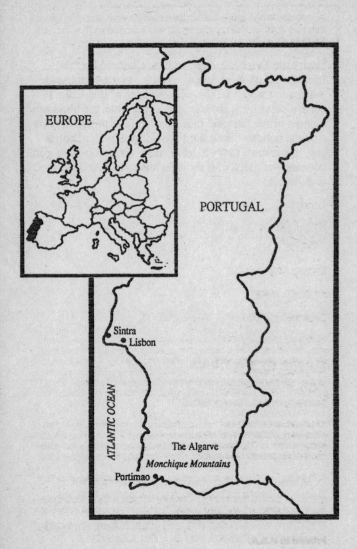

EUROPE

PORTUGAL

Sintra
Lisbon

ATLANTIC OCEAN

The Algarve
Monchique Mountains

Portimao

Dear Reader,

Each time I visit the Algarve I am charmed by the
friendliness of its people, the beauty of the countryside
whatever the season, the relaxing pace of life. Colors
seem clearer here; the sky is a deeper blue, the blossoms
a purer white, the sand more golden. The region may be
a prime holiday destination providing excellent hotels
and apartments, every kind of water sport, top-class golf
courses, yet much of it remains unspoiled. And the food
is delicious!

Enjoy!

Elizabeth Oldfield

Books by Elizabeth Oldfield

HARLEQUIN PRESENTS

Don't miss any of our special offers. Write to us at the
following address for information on our newest releases.

Harlequin Reader Service
U.S.: 3010 Walden Ave., P.O. Box 1325, Buffalo, NY 14269
Canadian: P.O. Box 609, Fort Erie, Ont. L2A 5X3

CHAPTER ONE

As SHE reached the crest of the hill, Ashley drew the baby buggy to a halt. Behind dark glasses, her hazel eyes gleamed and she smiled. No matter how many times she made the journey, this on-high vista proved endlessly fascinating. Below her, tucked into a natural bowl where a lush green valley met the aquamarine of the Atlantic Ocean, nestled the tiny fishing village of Praia do Carvoeiro. The squat houses shone a brilliant white in the August sunshine and their red-tiled roofs glittered. She saw washing swaying lazily in the breeze, balconies spilling with china-blue jacaranda blossoms, birdcages strung beneath eaves in order that their feathered occupants could enjoy the air. Ashley's smile widened. The decision, made six months ago, to uproot herself from England and move to the Algarve might not have been easy, but it had been the right one.

All of a sudden, the child in the buggy gave a squeal of delight.

'Mo' cars,' he pronounced, excitedly pointing a finger towards the foot of the hill where the lane met the village street in a T-junction.

'Lots of motor cars,' Ashley said wryly, for the bar of the T was packed bumper to bumper with stationary vehicles. '*Muito de tráfico.*'

Her son twisted to grin up at her from beneath his

7

white cotton sunhat. '*Tráfico*,' he repeated, with relish.

Thomas was motor-crazy, she thought, gazing fondly down at the small dungareed figure. Heaven for him meant them being given a lift in a girlfriend's second-hand Fiat and, whereas other toddlers of fifteen months or so usually toted teddy bears or other furry animals, he never went anywhere without taking along at least one toy car. Her eyes fell to the paint-peeled, much loved miniature moke which was clutched tight in his plump fist. Like now. Had this passion for anything on four wheels been inherited from his father? Ashley found herself wondering. She frowned. Such thoughts were always unsettling and she refused to spoil a perfect summer morning by dwelling on the matter now. Pushing her sunglasses higher up her short straight nose, she tucked a renegade wisp of pale honey-coloured hair back into her topknot, and started to walk again.

Although her descent down the steep incline took several minutes, the queue at the foot remained motionless. Praia do Carvoeiro's narrow winding streets had not been built with the car in mind, Ashley reflected as she walked along, let alone the beer waggon, the concrete mixer, the tourist coach. A one-way system meant that out of season hold-ups were rare, but in the peak summer months when the holidaymakers poured in by the dozens in their hire cars the village often became jammed. What was the trouble today? she wondered, as impatient horn blasts began to sound.

At the junction Ashley went right, making for the

square which, with its bars and cafés and entrance on to the golden sand arc of a beach, formed the focus of the small community. As she turned the corner, her lips curved. Two donkey carts, one piled high with hay, the other laden with cheap cooking utensils, had collided, and the road was strewn with aluminium kettles, ladles and pans. Little damage had been done, all it needed was for the cargo to be reassembled, but, while several tourists were rushing energetically around attempting to do this, the drivers of the carts had taken time off to chat. They were relaxed and puffing on cigarettes; it was clear that any responsibility for the inert procession which now crocodiled back out of the village failed to bother them. And neither did the cacophony of exasperated hoots which was soaring to a crescendo.

Amused by this demonstration of Portuguese *laissez-faire*, Ashley watched for a minute or two, then swung away to begin her shopping. She was heading for the *supermercado* when a flaxen-haired man with a teak-dark tan waved vigorously from beyond a group of onlookers on the opposite side of the square.

'Leif's coming,' she informed Thomas, as the man made his way across. 'Cross your fingers and hope he has another order for me.'

An ambitious Dane, Leif Haraldsen had been attracted to the Algarve by its business potential and the opportunity for water sports, and was now the owner of a thriving kitchen-installation company. Constantly on the look-out for ideas which might boost his trade, he had barely allowed Ashley time to launch her own one-girl operation before he had knocked at her door. The tiles which she painted possessed great potential in kitchen design, he had informed her. Their style and sophistication would appeal to the discerning customer. His prophecy had proved to be correct, for the trade he brought her way currently accounted for a good thirty per cent of her income. And income was important.

'Yesterday Senhora Rocha, the solicitor's wife, signed a contract for a de luxe kitchen,' Leif revealed, after they had exchanged greetings. 'Final details are still to be agreed, but I took along the usual samples of your work and it looks as though she'll want to incorporate feature tiles and maybe also a patterned frieze.'

Ashley grinned. 'Thanks.'

'Thank *you*,' he responded, in his clipped voice. 'That I'm able to offer specially designed, hand-painted tiling lifts my kitchens out of the ordinary and helps me to market them. We make a good team.' He slid an arm around her. 'And we could make an even better team if you'd give us half a chance.'

Her grin stiffened. In addition to being attracted to the Algarve, Leif Haraldsen was also attracted to her and, as the months passed, had begun to make his attraction increasingly plain. With deep blue eyes and springy fair hair, the athletic Dane would be the answer to many a maiden's prayer, yet while Ashley was grateful to have him as a friend and business associate she had no inclination for their relationship to deepen. Romantic attachments did not feature on her agenda.

'Yes,' she agreed, with an uneasy tug at the collar of the coral-pink shirt she wore with well-cut though much washed jeans.

'We do,' Leif insisted and, splaying his fingers at her waist, he drew her closer.

Ashley gritted her teeth. She objected to this invasion of her personal space. She did not appreciate being manhandled. But she did not want to — could not really afford to — offend him.

'It's two years since his father was killed — ' he continued, flicking a downwards glance at Thomas, who was engrossed in the pantomime in the centre of the square ' — and, while Simon's death was tragic, it's time to put it behind you.'

'I have,' she muttered.

'It's a crime for such a lovely young woman to live alone. You have needs which ought to be filled and — '

She stepped smartly aside. Enough was enough. She had no wish to be told about her needs. She had no wish to argue with Leif. All she wanted was to maintain their companionable, platonic and mutually beneficial business affiliation.

'Your kitchens obviously continue to be in great demand,' Ashley said.

The comment was made with the intention of changing the subject and, thanks to the Dane's interest in his commercial success, her ploy worked, for he nodded and proceeded to recite what sounded like a full two pages from his order book. He seemed about to move on to a third when Thomas gave a sudden yell.

'Mo' car,' he cried, semaphoring wildly and demanding her attention.

Ashley glanced up to see that, at long last, the donkey carts had shifted and the traffic had begun to flow. Some of the queue was syphoning off into a road signposted for Algar Seco, a bizarre coastal rock formation on the outskirts of the village, while other vehicles were following the one-way system and looping in and out of the square. The car which had caught the little boy's eye was a black 6-series BMW saloon — a car which possessed far more style and expensive panache than those which were normally seen around. It was waiting on the corner of the square, poised to enter.

'Hmm,' she acknowledged vaguely.

'*Big* mo' car,' Thomas emphasised, dissatisfied with such a lacklustre response.

'Very big,' Ashley agreed, as the BMW swung round in a perfectly described arc in front of them.

After so much delay and frustration it was being driven at speed, and so zipped across her vision in one swift-moving moment. At the sight of the driver, Ashley's hazel eyes flew wide. She froze. Memories fell down on her like stones. It *can't* be, an inner voice shrieked in violent protest. It *is*, another voice insisted. The car sped on and she stared, her gaze chained to the dark silhouette of the driver's head until the BMW turned a corner and vanished from sight.

Ashley fixed trembling hands tighter around the

pushbar of the buggy. Vitor d'Arcos was *here*? He had been so close she could have almost touched him. So near that, had he glanced sideways, he would have been bound to see her standing with Thomas. A storm broke loose in her head. Although two years had passed since that nightmare day when Simon had crashed on the Grand Prix circuit in Australia, Ashley had always known that, sooner or later, it must be her destiny to meet up with the tall, broad-shouldered Portuguese again. With the man who had been Simon's team-mate. But she did not want to have to confront him right now, she thought frantically. Not yet. Maybe she could be accused of cowardice, but she wasn't ready, wasn't prepared. Besides, she needed any meeting to be at *her* bidding, take place at *her* chosen venue, be conducted on *her* terms. Mustering every possible advantage — no matter how great or how small — was essential.

'My business is here to stay,' Leif declared, beside her. 'Unlike some. For instance, did you know that the guy who bought up all the land around your place has gone bust?'

Ashley blinked. 'Sorry?'

'He's been declared bankrupt.'

In a strenuous effort, she dragged her mind back to the present. 'Are you sure?' she enquired, as her companion's statement sunk in. 'After months of no one coming near, last week a team of men arrived and spent days walking around and surveying, so —' she made a face ' — I assumed work on the dreaded *parque aquático* was about to start.'

Ashley lived in what had originally been a farmhouse, a couple of miles outside Praia do Carvoeiro. The single-storey grey stone building stood amid fields where vines and figs used to grow in abundance, but which had been left to run wild and were now covered in bright carpets of wild flowers. While the rural location possessed great charm it was isolated and at times Ashley felt a little bit vulnerable, so when a local builder had acquired the land she had been pleased. He would erect houses, she would have neighbours, Thomas would be able to play with their children. Perfect. However, she had soon discovered that the man's plans were far more exotic. A complex of swimming-pools, splash pools and towering chutes was to be built on three sides of her home, with a vast car park to the front. Ashley had rushed hotfoot to the area planning office to object, but had been told, sorry, she was too late and permission had already been granted.

'I'm positive,' Leif replied. 'No name's been mentioned, but I understand an international construction company has bought out the business lock, stock and barrel, so now the *parque aquático* will be their baby. I imagine they'll be keen to start work as soon as possible in the hope of having it ready for next season, and with their resources you can be sure——'

Ashley's concentration wavered and her thoughts travelled back to the man in the car. Where was Vitor d'Arcos now? she wondered. Speeding away from the village never to return—or parked just around the corner? He wasn't going to abruptly reappear, was he? He hadn't seen an image in the corner of his eye, belatedly realised who it could be, and was making his way back on foot to investigate? No, no, she was certain he had not spotted her.

'So I'm afraid the only thing you can do is grin and bear it,' Leif said, in what was obviously a finale.

Ashley looked blank. She had, it seemed, missed whole tracts of his spiel.

'Er—I guess,' she agreed.

'Are you feeling all right?' the Dane asked, leaning closer. 'You look a little pale.'

She summoned up a smile. 'I'm fine. Time's passing and I must go. I look forward to hearing what Senhora Rocha decides. See you again,' she gabbled, and strode away.

Both the local people and the expatriate community had been happy to befriend the pretty blonde newcomer and her infant son, with the result that whenever Ashley came down to the village she spent a good proportion of her time chatting. Not today. Her responses to the usual chorus of cheery greetings were half-hearted; all she could focus on was Vitor d'Arcos. The shock of seeing him again—and in Praia do Carvoeiro! It was something she had never anticipated, a circumstance which filled her with alarm. As she called in at the *supermercado*, toured the fruit and vegetable market, bought chicken legs from the Dutch butcher, a kaleidoscope of questions formed and reformed itself in her head. How would Vitor have reacted if he *had* seen her? What would he have said? Lances of remembrance pierced her heart, and she flinched. Would he have flung the bitter allegations and repeated the damning indictment of her which he had made at the time of Simon's death?

Whoa, girl. Calm down. Think again, Ashley told herself as, having checked that the purchases stashed in the buggy's basket were secure, she started the return climb up the lane. Are you one hundred per cent certain that the man in the car actually *was* Vitor d'Arcos? Could you swear on oath? She chewed at her lip. All she had had was a split-second glimpse of a profile as the car had swept past, followed by a fast retreating view of the back of the man's head as he had accelerated away, and what kind of a basis was that for identification? None. Everyone made mistakes and today she had been mistaken. Her eyes had played tricks and her imagination had run wild. Gone haywire. Some mental quirk had had her jumping—wham, bam!— to an instinctive conclusion, but it had been the wrong conclusion. Portugal was full of males with strong proud features and heads of thick dark hair, and the lone driver had been a stranger. Someone she did not know. Someone with no input into her past and without any possible power to damage her future.

Ashley's spirits lifted. She smiled. Her attack of skittering panic had been unnecessary and foolish. After all, Vitor d'Arcos had no reason to decide to visit the end-of-the-road, tucked-away village of Praia do Carvoeiro. . .did he?

* * *

When they returned to the farmhouse, it was lunch-time. Ashley scrambled eggs which she and Thomas ate outside on the leafy vine-shaded terrace and then, following her regular routine, she put the little boy down for his nap. Now, with luck, she would have one toddler-free hour, she thought as she stripped off her jeans and changed into her working gear. A busy profitable hour.

Off to one side of the house stood a low white-washed building originally used as stables and later as a garage, but which, after much industrious clearing, cleaning and the application of repeated coats of apricot-white emulsion now did duty as studio-cum-shop. Here Ashley designed her tiles, painted and fired them in a small kiln. Here she displayed them. The work which awaited was a panel depicting typical Algarve scenes—fishing boats beside a jetty, orange groves, a row of picturesque village houses—which had been commissioned to grace the lobby of a nearby hotel, and now she mixed colours. The tip of her tongue protruding from between her teeth in concentration, she started to shade in the outline of a filigreed chimney.

Fifteen minutes later, Ashley heard the sound of a vehicle drawing to a halt on the unmade road at the front of the house. She tilted her head towards the open door. Could this be Leif, calling to advise that the Rocha kitchen would include her tiles and asking if she would confer with the solicitor's wife? Or had a tourist picked up one of the cards she had lavishly distributed around the village shops and arrived to buy a souvenir?

After hastily tidying her display shelves, Ashley continued to paint, but no one appeared. She gave an exasperated sigh. On the wall outside she had fixed a large notice which clearly indicated that here was the shop, and for someone to miss it they would need to be exceedingly short-sighted—or dozy. Jettisoning her brush, she went out into the still sultry heat of the afternoon. A hand was raised to shade her eyes and she looked around. There was no one in sight. No sound, except the lazy drone of the cicadas in the trees.

A tiny spring of fear uncoiled itself. As usual, she had left the back door ajar, so—failing to realise that anyone was around—could whoever it was who had arrived have entered her home? Might they be rifling through her belongings? Had they discovered her sleeping child? Her heart full of foreboding and with all her motherly instincts on red alert, Ashley sprang forward. She needed to get to Thomas. The intruder must be ousted. She had sprinted over the drive and was halfway across the stone-flagged terrace when a figure appeared around the corner of the house. Ashley's run came to a startled panting stop. It was a tall man with an aquiline nose and thick dark hair. He wore a charcoal-grey business suit, with a pristine white shirt and maroon silk tie. In navigating the corner he had walked from shade straight into the blinding-white glare of the sun and, as her gallop had ceased, so the man also stopped dead, apparently dazzled despite the protection of a pair of sepia-tinted gold-rimmed glasses.

Ashley's stomach pitched and tossed. She felt *ill*.

In persuading herself that her identification was faulty she had, she acknowledged, been the oh, so eager victim of wishful thinking. Indeed, her doubt could be described as wilful blindness. She knew that there was one compelling reason why Vitor d'Arcos should visit Praia do Carvoeiro and yet, instead of facing up to the possibility and planning a strategy, she had denied it. But how had he discovered her whereabouts? Why, after two years, should he suddenly zero in out of the blue? And—the crunch—now that he had realised the truth, what did he intend to do about it? As answers to the last question jibber-jabbered in her head, Ashley straightened. Whatever he might fling at her this time, she would not sit bowed and tongue-tied. She would not be tyrannised. Yet when her visitor stepped a couple of paces forward as though requiring a closer look, it needed all her courage not to back away.

'Ashley,' he murmured, in a smoky-accented voice which seemed so familiar.

Her heart lurched into an erratic beat. She had convinced herself that the intense *impact* which Vitor d'Arcos had once had on her had been a much exaggerated memory, the figment of an overheated imagination. It was not so. Six feet two of perfectly conditioned muscle and bone, the ex-racing driver was a man of presence, a man of grandeur, a man who, despite her alarm, was making a very odd sensation career through her.

'Good afternoon. *Boa—boa tarde*,' Ashley stammered.

An offensive must be launched, she thought feverishly. His verbal rockets would doubtless already be primed, but she must defuse them by getting in first and establishing that the woman he faced today was a woman of determination, a woman prepared to fight, a woman who would be a fearsome opponent in any battle. What did she say? A search was made for an apt sock-it-to-him opening remark, yet nothing came.

'What are you doing here?' Vitor enquired. 'Why are you in Portugal? How do you come to be in Praia do Carvoeiro?'

Perplexed, Ashley looked at him, then it registered that as she had been astonished to see him so he was equally stunned to see her. Peals of deliriously relieved laughter threatened to burst from her throat. Vitor d'Arcos did not know the truth. He had not sought out her address. He had not tracked her down. Whatever the reason for his presence here, it had nothing to do with her! Ashley offered up a fervent thanks. So she did not need to go on the offensive and was not required to fight. All she had to do was tack together her shattered composure, offer a few polite words — and get rid of him as soon as possibe.

'This is my house,' she said.

Thick dark brows soared above the sepia-tinted glasses. 'Yours? You're the owner?' His brows lowered into a frown. 'I remember you once told me how you spent a lot of time on the Algarve when you were young,' Vitor said, 'but I had no idea which area you came to.'

'It was here. The house used to belong to my grandfather, who let my parents use it as a holiday home,' Ashley explained, 'but he died last winter and left it to me. Unfortunately his failing health meant he couldn't visit much in recent years, and my folks spent their holidays elsewhere, so the house had become neglected. I've done as much as I can to make it comfortable, but, among other things, it needs a modern bathroom, a new roof and all the windows replaced. As soon as the cash is available I shall have the jobs done, though when that will be——' Ashley stopped short. Whenever she felt nervous she had a tendency to chatter, but there was no need to give chapter and verse. 'I live here,' she confirmed.

'But, unlike your grandfather, you live here permanently,' Vitor said.

Maybe it was his inflexion or the lilt of his accent, yet the remark sounded more like a statement than a question.

'That's right,' she replied. 'I've been here for six months.'

Vitor removed his sunglasses, folded them and slid them into the top pocket of his jacket. When the peat-brown eyes fixed on hers again, their level gaze showed he had recovered from his astonishment at seeing her. It had not taken him long, Ashley thought wryly. But Vitor d'Arcos had always been mentally strong and his time as a racing driver meant his reflexes had been honed to the micro-second.

'You sell hand-painted tiles,' he pronounced, and

this time there could be no doubt that he was stating what he knew to be a fact.

Ashley shot him a cautious glance from beneath her fringe of thick dark lashes. Vitor might not have been aware that she occupied the house, yet he had amassed some items of information about her. Why? she wondered, once again on her guard. Of what interest could her present lifestyle be to him?

'I do,' she agreed briefly.

'It must be very different from travelling the globe as the whiz-kid design director for one of Britain's foremost home décor companies,' he observed.

'It is, though I'm enjoying running my own business. I may not possess any status or receive a substantial monthly pay cheque, but to have my trade grow entirely through my own efforts is one heck of a kick. And my trade's growing fast. I've only been operational for four months and yet already people are beginning to seek me out. The other day a woman rang from as far away as——' Ashley stopped, aware of chattering again. 'Times change, people change,' she finished.

Vitor lifted a brow. 'Dramatically, in some ways.'

'Sorry?'

'I've never seen you so. . .casual.'

Ashley imagined how she must look. Once she had taken care with her clothes, her make-up, her hair, but now. . . Her working gear comprised an oversized boat-necked T-shirt which had a habit of slipping off one shoulder, frayed denim shorts and flip-flops. After showering this morning she had brushed her lashes with mascara and that still remained, but the rosy lip-gloss, which had been her only other concession to cosmetics, was long gone. As for the hair which used to be trimmed by a top London stylist and had swung in a smooth shoulder-skimming bob, it had not been cut for months and was now bundled unceremoniously on to the top of her head. Ashley's hackles rose. While she knew she must resemble a ragamuffin, she did not appreciate the reminder.

'I'd have got out the padded shoulders and the four-inch heels had I known you were going to appear looking like someone whom Central Casting had sent to play——' her gaze flicked over his well-groomed appearance and immaculate suit '—the Wall Street tycoon,' she said astringently.

Vitor's mouth tweaked. 'I'll tell my tailor you approve, but you're reading me wrong. I think you look great.' His gaze touched on her high cheek-bones, her mouth with its full sensuous lower lip and shorter, bowed upper one, the peach-smooth and lightly tanned complexion. 'You still have the kind of face which ought to be in the business of launching ships.' His eyes made a significant dip and he waited a couple of beats before adding, 'And the kind of body which has been known to drive men wild. So you're happy living on the Algarve?' he continued.

Hot colour scorched her cheeks. Why did he have to make such a provocative remark? Ashley wondered furiously. Why must he remind her of what had once happened between them and which now— her heart tightened—could never be removed? Yet, despite his reference to the past, Vitor had not sounded hostile. On the contrary, his manner seemed genial and. . .conciliatory.

'I'm very happy,' she said.

'You've made friends?'

'Lots. Twice a week I meet up with a group of other young mothers for a baby afternoon and——'

'You have men friends?' Vitor interrupted.

Ashley frowned. That was none of his business.

'Why are you here?' she demanded, ignoring the query and deciding that, from now on, if anyone was to conduct an interrogation it would be her.

Vitor smiled the slow crooked smile which had once had his female fans attempting to push their telephone numbers—sometimes accompanied by intimate items of underwear—into his hand.

'I've come to discuss a deal I'd like to do with you,' he said.

'Discuss a deal with me?' Ashley echoed. She had been wrong; his presence *was* to do with her. 'What kind of a deal?' she asked suspiciously.

Vitor eased open the buttons on his jacket with long fingers. 'Perhaps we could talk about it indoors where it's cooler?' he suggested, with a nod towards the house.

Ashley had a shivery moment. She did not want Vitor d'Arcos inside her home. She did not want him anywhere near it. Deal or no mysterious deal, now that it had been established that he had not tracked her down all she wanted was for him to go. Very soon.

'My workshop would be more convenient,' she declared, and hastily fashioned an excuse. 'I was in the middle of painting a tile and I'd like to finish it before it dries. It's this way,' she said, and, swivelling on her heel, she marched smartly back across the drive.

'Aye, aye, Captain,' Vitor d'Arcos murmured, behind her.

On reaching the workshop, Ashley installed herself behind her table. Had she scuttled behind it? she wondered, as she filled her brush with colour. Probably — yet, with Vitor's presence seeming to fill the room, a sense of self-preservation had insisted she erect some barrier between them.

In her haste, the wayward T-shirt had slipped, and she hooked it back on to her shoulder. 'Well?' she demanded.

He nodded towards her display. 'Mind if I take a look?'

'Carry on,' Ashley replied, somewhat tersely.

She was all set to paint, but when Vitor slid his hands into his trouser pockets and, with jacket flaring back, strolled across to inspect the items which she had for sale, her gaze compulsively followed him. As he had seen no change in her, so she could see little difference in him. The lines on his brow might be etched a touch more deeply and there was the stray glint of silver among the thick dark hair at his temples, but Vitor d'Arcos remained. . .not handsome — his nose was too arrogant and his jaw too hard-hewn for that — but an arresting-looking man.

As she was gazing at him, he turned to study a different row of tiles and a shaft of sunlight illuminated the left side of his face. Cut into the sultry gold of his skin she saw a thin white line which zigzagged down from beside his eye, along his cheek-bone, to his jaw. Ashley's throat constricted. The scar would be a legacy of the injuries which he had received when attempting to haul Simon from the wreckage of his car. The injuries which had been forgotten when he had levelled his furious accusations.

'You have a great sense of style,' Vitor declared.

'Thanks,' Ashley said, and started to paint.

'Your tiles are the reason why I'm here today,' he said.

His hands remained in his trouser pockets and, as Vitor stood with long legs apart, the charcoal-grey flannel was stretched tight across his thighs. She wished he would not stand like that, Ashley thought edgily. It was too *male*. She also wished he would stop talking in riddles and make sense.

'You want to buy some?' she hazarded.

He shook his head. 'I've taken over a local building firm which has unfortunately gone belly-up,' Vitor told her, 'and included among their assets is a plot of a sizeable number of acres which encompasses your property.'

Ashley looked at him in confusion. 'So now you own the land?' Her painting was abandoned. 'But. . . In that case. . .' A frantic attempt was made to recall what Leif had said. 'The international company is your company?' she protested.

He nodded. 'You won't remember, but all the time I was racing I also ran a construction business.'

She did remember. She remembered every single thing Vitor d'Arcos had ever said to her, Ashley thought, in grim self-mockery. So she knew that before being coaxed into motor racing at the belated age of thirty Vitor had qualified as an architect and gained a Harvard business degree. She knew that, after an initial period of gaining experience with a leading European firm, he had set up on his own. She knew that in between Formula One obligations he had, amazingly, managed to keep his construction interests afloat. But what she did *not* know was what had happened to those interests — or to him — since Simon's death, apart from the fact that Vitor had immediately retired from racing. At first the information lack had been due to an instinctive veering away from the man who had caused her so much hurt and distress, but now it was more a matter of her rarely spending money on a paper and not having a television.

'And your business has become a major concern?' Ashley enquired.

Vitor nodded. 'It could have been major much earlier — I had the know-how and had already done the groundwork — but when I was racing there wasn't the time, nor did I have the surplus energy to allow the business its head. However, for the past two years I've dedicated myself to it in total and, like yours, my trade has mushroomed.' He allowed himself a small satisfied smile. 'Now I have offices in New York, San Paulo and Lisbon.'

'Plus one in the centre of Praia do Carvoeiro,' she reminded him.

'True, though it's only a yard with a three-room building, so as soon as possible we shall sell up and move to something bigger.'

Move out of the village, Ashley begged silently. Move to a place many miles away. As the big boss you won't be at the Carvoeiro office too often, but it would be easier for my peace of mind if you were not there at all!

'In Portugal we've been restricting our developments to Lisbon and the North,' Vitor went on, 'but recently my board and I made the decision to bring the d'Arcos style to the Algarve.'

D'Arcos style? She cast him a scathing look. He made it sound as though he would be doing the region a favour, not erecting a gaudy, intrusive, unaesthetic and, in her opinion, entirely superfluous tourist attraction!

'And for your debut you're "developing" ——' the word dripped acid ' — the acres of land around me?' Ashley enquired, stalking out from behind the table to confront him.

'We are,' Vitor said. 'However ——'

She cut him short. 'With sea views to the south and the Monchique mountains to the north, this is a delightful stretch of countryside. You agree?' she demanded.

'I do, though ——'

'The guy who's gone bust didn't have an environmentally friendly bone in his body, but I would have thought better of you,' Ashley declared. 'You're an architect, someone who's supposed to improve this planet, not festoon it with ill-placed coils of lurid metal. Don't you care that, because of the elevated position, all the chutes and flumes and the other pipework will be visible for miles around? It *will*,' she insisted, when Vitor seemed about to protest. 'I've driven past these water parks and they're invariably painted turquoise or bright blue.' Ashley shuddered. 'Don't you care that the roads here are country roads unsuitable for heavy traffic and will be ruined by all the cars which descend? Doesn't it matter to you that in a place where you can now hear birdsong there'll be pop music blaring and loudspeakered announcements from morning to night? No, it does not!'

'Oh, my,' Vitor murmured, the corner of his mouth twitching as though he found her vehemence entertaining.

Ashley glared. 'What about the trees which will be felled?' she carried on. 'What about the natural contours of the land which will need to be flattened? What about the intrusion which *I'm* destined to suffer?'

'I was mistaken, you have changed,' he said. 'You're more assertive and——' his dark eyes fell to the impassioned rise and fall of her chest beneath the cotton T-shirt '—your breasts are fuller.'

The remark knocked her askew. Speechless for a moment, Ashley could not decide whether to scream, cross her arms protectively over her chest, or to hit him.

'I know that water parks provide lots of people with lots of fun, but there are two others within fifty miles of here so there's absolutely no need for

another one,' she continued, her cheeks flaming.
'I've already informed the authorities of my disap-
proval but, because permission had been granted, I
went no further. However this time, whether or not
a change of ownership makes any difference to that
permission, I intend to lodge an official complaint. I
shall go to the planning office and demand an
interview with their top man first thing in the morning. I shall also get busy organising a local petition!
So don't think that——'

'Would you mind if I had a turn to talk?' Vitor
enquired mildly.

Ashley glowered. 'Go ahead.'

'We're not constructing a water park,' he said,
demolishing her tirade in one short sentence.

She stared at him. 'No?'

'Like you, I believe it would be a sin to site one
here.'

'Oh.' Ashley felt a complete idiot. 'So what are
you intending to—to do with the land?' she faltered.

'Build villas. Five-bedroom, double-garaged prop-
erties, individually designed and standing in plots of
well over an acre. Each villa will have a landscaped
garden which retains the natural contours and the
majority of the trees. They also come with a pool,
barbecue area and jacuzzi.'

'Classy,' she muttered, thinking that, while she
rebelled against *his* firm being involved, villas were
what she had originally hoped for.

'They will be,' Vitor said, 'which is why we wish
to buy your house.'

Her hazel eyes opened wide. 'Buy my house?' Ashley queried.

'My surveyors have drawn up the plans and it's going to be virtually mid-centre of the site.'

'So?'

Vitor smiled his slow crooked smile. 'So we'd rather you weren't here.'

CHAPTER TWO

ASHLEY's lips jammed together. Now she knew why Vitor's attitude had been conciliatory. It had had nothing to do with the past and everything to do with him wanting to oust her from her home. Acting in steely self-interest, he had been intent on softening her up before he pounced!

'You reckon an old building will jar with your luxury villas, so you want to buy it and demolish it?' she asked, her voice frigid.

Vitor strolled over to the open door to look out at the house with its quaint latticed windows, its white-painted shutters, the walls awash with waterfalls of crimson bougainvillaea.

'On the contrary, a house of such character can only add to the development,' he replied. 'Paulo's suggested we should turn it into a small club for residents, and, from what I've seen, it seems like a good idea.' He turned to face her. 'The reason why we wish to purchase the property is that we obviously aren't happy to have a business concern operating in the midst of a residential area — which is why I've come to open negotiations by making you an offer.'

'No, thanks,' Ashley said.

'You haven't heard what it is,' Victor observed equably.

'Even so——'

'What we propose to do,' he said, in a voice which allowed no argument, 'is ask an estate agent, of your choice, to make an independent valuation of the property and then add five million *escudos* on top; at today's exchange rate that's. . .' He did quick mental arithmetic and named a large sum. 'The money is a bona fide payment in thanks for your co-operation and to compensate you for the upheaval. In addition, my company will pick up the tab for all legal and moving expenses. I realise that before making any commitment you'll want to take advice, but perhaps you could let me have your initial response?'

'I'm not interested,' she said, and walked past him and out into the sunshine.

Vitor followed. 'It's a good deal,' he said.

'I'm not disputing that. However, firstly, I happen to like living here,' Ashley told him, 'and secondly, I fail to see how me running my workshop is going to bother anyone.'

'What about the tourists who come up from the village on foot or arrive in their cars to take a look at your goods?' he demanded. 'Won't they be a bother? Won't they disrupt the tranquillity of the neighbourhood? Won't they *jar*?'

'No, because there are not that many.'

Vitor cast her an impatient look. 'You've already said how rapidly your trade is growing and according to Paulo——'

'Who is Paulo?' Ashley interrupted.

'The guy who's in charge of the development and

who'll be running the office. He moved into an apartment in the village a week ago.'

'It was Paulo who told you that the owner of the house painted tiles?'

'Yes. He spotted your sign,' Vitor said, with a nod towards it, 'so he's been speaking to the locals and asking a few questions.'

'What you mean is, one of your spies has assembled a secret dossier of facts about me,' she said accusingly.

Exasperation glittered in his dark brown eyes. 'As your property happens to be slap-bang in the middle of our site, it seemed like common sense to discover what went on here. And it was fortunate we did, because what do we find? A thriving cottage industry. According to Paulo,' he carried on, 'in just about every single shop in Praia do Carvoeiro there are cards issuing an open invitation for the world and his wife to come and view your tiles, which——'

'The cards have only raked in a few customers,' Ashley said. 'Although more would be welcome, I'm too far off the beaten track. The bulk of my sales I get through commissions.'

'Presumably whoever gives you the commissions must come here to see the kind of things you do?' Vitor enquired. 'And visit to check on progress from time to time? Visit in their cars?'

'Well. . .yes.'

'And your supplies——' he swept a golden-skinned hand towards a stack of unglazed tiles which sat outside the workshop door '—will be delivered by truck. Surely it doesn't require a degree in sociology to realise that people who invest their hard-earned cash in a quality house in a quality development are not going to be over the moon at having that kind of to-ing and fro-ing take place outside their front gates?'

'You make it sound as though there are juggernauts forever roaming around,' Ashley said tetchily. 'My supplies come by van and that's only once or twice a month.'

'Even so, there *is* a degree of commercial activity,' Vitor insisted.

'Even so, I am not willing to sell,' she retorted.

His lean face darkened and he muttered something in Portuguese beneath his breath. Something which she failed to translate, but which could be recognised as distinctly unflattering.

'Suppose I increase my offer?' he suggested.

Ashley shook her head. 'No.'

'And I used to think you were one smart cookie,' Vitor rasped.

'Excuse me?'

'Compared to many other parts of Europe, property in Portugal is relatively low-priced so the extra amount of money would lift you into a different, far higher bracket. You told me the house is in need of attention; move and you can move to a place which is in excellent order *and* in a more central position where you'll be able to attract more customers,' he said, treading a verbal tightrope between head-banging irritation and reasoned appeal.

Ashley glanced towards her home. While the scenario he had painted held some undeniable attractions, she was not tempted. Vitor d'Arcos might have altered the direction of her life once, but he would not be allowed to do so again. Not if she could help it, she thought fiercely. Now she made the decisions, now she was in control, and if, at some future date, she should sell the farmhouse it would be because it was *her* choice and not to accommodate him. Besides, he was over-reacting. The workshop would not cause *that* much disruption. A shadow crossed her features. But perhaps her main reason for staying put was that, if she accepted what was plainly a generous offer, she would feel herself placed under some kind of an obligation and put morally in his debt. No, thanks. Anything which involved her in unnecessary enmeshment with Vitor d'Arcos would be sturdily fended off.

'No,' Ashley said again.

His look was as chill as the Arctic. 'I'd be grateful if you could deign to spare my proposition a full thirty seconds of considered thought.'

She sneaked a glance at her watch and another glance towards the house. Thomas was due to awake. Sometimes the little boy climbed from his cot and played for a while indoors, though more usually he toddled out on to the terrace, in search of her and a drink

'There's nothing to consider,' she said. 'I have no wish to sell and that's final.' Her gaze took a pointed veer down the drive. 'Goodbye.'

Vitor folded his arms across his chest. 'I remember your impetuous, spur-of-the-moment streak,' he said.

Ashley's heart cramped. She knew exactly what he meant, could recall in graphic detail the event to which he was referring. It was on the tip of her tongue to answer this blow below the belt with a savage 'ditto!' but there was not the time, nor did she have the inclination to resurrect the past right now.

'You're taking this matter of my workshop far too seriously,' she declared. 'No one's going to throw a fit over the occasional visitor and a fortnightly van.'

'Your commercial activities will disturb the neighbourhood,' he repeated.

Ashley's eyes returned to the house. She listened. Had Thomas called? No, it was her imagination.

'That might be your view, but it's not mine,' she said. 'Now, if you'll excuse me——'

'Because there were telephone calls to make and various matters which needed my attention, I was up at dawn this morning,' Vitor told her. 'Then I drove almost two hundred miles down from Lisboa in order to visit whoever it was who owned this house.'

'You thought that if you turned up in the smart suit and with the laser-beam smile you'd wow them into panting agreement?' Ashley enquired, before he could get any further.

His jaw hardened. 'I thought the owner might appreciate me taking the time and trouble to approach them in person,' he bit out. 'I wanted to show that we cared about their predicament and wished to conduct a genial and mutually satisfying transaction, and I thought the head of the company bothering to put in an appearance might do that.'

'Especially as the head of the company happens to be the well-known ex-Formula One maestro, Vitor d'Arcos,' she observed coolly. 'Who could resist an approach from him?'

His hands clenched into fists. He seemed sorely tempted to throttle her.

'It's two years since I last lined up on a grid,' Vitor said, 'and since then I've refused to give interviews and avoided all contact with the media. Stay out of the limelight and you're quickly forgotten. Formula-One addicts may remember me, but I can assure you that to the public at large I'm just another average, ordinary guy.'

Ashley said nothing. While he clearly believed what he was saying, and while his image might have faded from the general consciousness, Vitor d'Arcos was too commanding, too vital, too much the male sexual animal to ever be considered ordinary.

'I drive down hoping to open negotiations with the house owner,' he continued, 'spend time with Paulo in the office, then grab a bite of lunch before I return to Lisboa, but——'

'You're going back to Lisbon today?' she cut in, surprised by such a gruelling schedule.

'I am. But what happens when I arrive in Praia do Carvoeiro?' Vitor went on. 'First I get stuck in the mother of all traffic jams, and then I'm confronted by a woman who blocks her ears to reason and is a complete and utter pain in the ass.'

'You say jump and I'm supposed to ask how high?' Ashley challenged.

'You're supposed to give my proposition some serious thought,' he shot back. 'I don't expect an immediate answer. I'll confirm my offer in writing and when you receive the letter you can go and talk it over with an estate agent and your solicitor.'

'There's no need.'

He slammed the flat of his hand hard against the wall of the workshop, making her jump.

'What do you want me to do,' Vitor demanded, 'get down on my knees and beg?'

Ashley gave a small smile. The blood which flowed in his veins meant that, as well as expressing his emotions with the dramatic use of his hands, Vitor d'Arcos was a proud man—and she doubted he had ever begged anyone for anything in his entire life.

'You could give it a whirl,' she said.

He frowned. 'Refusing to consider my offer isn't some kind of revenge for what I said in Adelaide?' he asked guardedly. 'If so, I want to apologise for my timing. To confront you at that particular moment was deplorable.' His frown deepened. 'I was a son of a bitch.'

'Yes, you were,' Ashley agreed blisteringly.

'My only excuse is that it was a traumatic incident and I was in shock.'

'But your opinion hasn't changed?'

Vitor's eyes met hers in a steady look. 'No.'

'Revenge isn't an issue,' Ashley told him, her tone incisive. 'And, whatever you may think, I have absolutely no problem with the circumstances of Simon's death.'

He was silent for a moment. 'Then why do you have to be so cussed?' he enquired.

'I'm not.'

'You damn well are! All I'm asking is that you take time to weigh up the deal I'm offering and —— Do you have a licence?' Vitor questioned abruptly.

'A licence for what?'

'To conduct a business out of these premises.'

As his eyes locked with hers, Ashley's colour rose and she began to feel harassed. Simon had once told her how if a Formula One driver blinked during a race it was the same as him driving thirty yards with his eyes shut, and Vitor's stare was unrelenting.

'Er — not exactly,' she mumbled.

'Which means?' he demanded.

'Well, just before I set up my workshop I sent off the application form to the appropriate office,' Ashley explained, 'but there was no acknowledgement. After about a month I rang and was told I'd be hearing something soon, and when I didn't I phoned again a month or so later and was told the same. But since then nothing's happened and ——'

'You've forgotten about it?' he demanded, when she spread her hands.

She nodded. Why hadn't she told a white lie and claimed she had a licence? Ashley wondered. Chances were he would have taken her at her word. But as well as her being uncomfortable with lying, her eyes had been trapped by the intensity of his gaze and telling him anything less than the truth, the whole truth, had seemed impossible.

'Everything official here seems to be tied up in red tape, so although it's taking a long time I'm sure the licence is being processed,' she declared defiantly.

Vitor eased down the knot of his tie. 'Four months is one hell of a delay, even for Portugal,' he observed. 'And your form could have been lost. Though lost or not, as you've never received any official sanction there must be a strong case to be made for claiming that you're trading illegally.' He gave a wolfish grin. 'Instead of you complaining to the authorities about my supposd *parque aquático*, perhaps I should complain about your workshop.'

Despite the heat, Ashley went cold. Was she breaking the law? If Vitor reported her might she be taken to court and fined? Could he have her business closed down?

'Is that a threat?' she enquired, adopting a painstakingly careless tone which was meant to conceal her trepidation.

'What do you think?'

'That's not an answer,' she protested.

'It's as good as you're going to get,' he said silkily.

Ashley picked agitatedly at the frayed leg of her shorts. She was handling the situation all wrong. Vitor had arrived with amicability in mind, albeit a self-serving amicability, and how had she responded? By being stubbornly obstructive and making snappy remarks. Yet while she had no intention of surrendering her home it would be foolish to let the atmosphere between them become *too* acrimonious. Not only did she need Vitor's goodwill now, but she could need it some time in the future; so turning him into an outright no-holds-barred enemy was shortsighted. . .and potentially dangerous.

'I'm sorry you're miffed because I don't want to sell and I'm sorry our views on the nuisance value of my workshop conflict,' Ashley said, 'but why don't we wait until the villas are occupied and take a vote among the owners? Then if they're anti I'll move.' She shone her most fetching smile, a smile which had once wowed captains of industry and beguiled all her clients. 'OK?'

'To use your favourite word — no,' Vitor replied.

Her smile faded. 'No?'

'You need me to spell it? N. O.'

Ashley looked at the house again. Why must he argue? Why couldn't he simply accept that she was not about to defer to his wishes and *go*? Go before Thomas made an entrance, which had to be imminent.

'Then all we can do is act like civilised adults and agree to differ,' she said, hearing herself sound like an agony aunt trotting out hackneyed advice.

'I may be civilised and adult; you I have strong doubts about,' Vitor responded curtly, and, taking a white handkerchief from his pocket, he wiped a sheen of perspiration from his brow.

Ashley reassembled her fetching smile. 'All right, send me your letter, and I promise to reconsider and let you have my reply as soon as possible.'

'You're humouring me,' he said.

'It isn't carved in stone that we have to fight about this,' she protested, wanting their meeting to end on a genial note, but mainly wanting it to end. *Now*.

In her agitation, her T-shirt had slipped again, and Vitor stretched out a hand.

'You mean we should make love, not war?' he enquired, brushing his fingertips across the smooth, tanned roundness of her exposed shoulder.

She had not meant that, Ashley thought frantically, at least not in the way his husky intonation was making it sound, not how the look in his dark eyes seemed to imply. She knew she should reply with some light-hearted quip which would set everything down on a matter-of-fact level and make her meaning plain, but quips were beyond her. All she could focus on was Vitor's touch, on the casual caress which was making an electric awareness dart across her skin. Ashley swallowed. She told herself to step away, but her legs refused to move. What was the matter with her? she wondered. She found no difficulty in detaching herself from Leif's advances, so why did she seem pathologically incapable of breaking contact now?

'I mean we can at least part ami — amicably,' Ashley stammered.

'Part as friends?'

She did not like having her personal space violated, she reminded herself in desperation, yet Vitor did not violate. Instead, his touch felt like bliss.

'Y — yes,' she got out.

'Then goodbye, friend,' Vitor said, and, cupping

two large hands around her shoulders, he drew her towards him and kissed her.

His lips were warm and soft, their touch light. Startled, Ashley opened her mouth to protest, but as she did his lips parted too. Their breath mingled; she felt the probe of his tongue against hers, absorbed the clean taste of him. Excitement streaked through her. A heat began to grow. It's happening again, she thought bemusedly, that wild-fire feeling. So break away, dumbo, instructed a voice in her head. You know what it led to before. You've learned your lesson, and how! Yet Ashley remained immobile.

Vitor's arms slid around her back, drawing her closer, and his kiss deepened. The feel of him, the taste of him, was like a drug, one which she believed she had kicked, but which, she was now discovering, continued to exert a ruthless grip.

'Mama!'

The cry acted like cold water, flung in her face and bringing her to her senses. Pushing free, Ashley spun round to see Thomas scampering merrily out barefoot on to the terrace. His brown curls were tousled and his cheeks were still flushed from sleep. Thank goodness you've rescued me, she thought, yet hard on the heels of her relief came dismay. She had been determined to avoid Vitor setting eyes on the child, but now——

'Hello, my love,' Ashley said, and ran forward to sweep him up into her arms and bury his head against her shoulder. 'I have to go,' she told her visitor, with a speedy smile. 'Bye.'

'I knew you'd had a son, but I didn't realise he was in the house,' Vitor said. 'As you were working and you run a business, I assumed you must leave him with a babyminder.'

Her flight faltered. Caring for Thomas herself was something which she felt very strongly about.

'Don't you think he's rather young to be farmed out all day and every day?' Ashley demanded.

'I do. However——'

'And so do I. Before he was born I decided he would come first and that, if it was at all possible, I'd be at home with him throughout his early years.'

'You felt that as he didn't have a father he deserved a full-time mother?' Vitor suggested.

She bobbed a brusque head. 'During the day I only paint when he's asleep, and sometimes for the extra hour if he's happy playing beside me. Most of my work I do in the evenings when he's in bed,' Ashley explained. 'Now, if you don't mind I must——'

'Aren't you going to let me have a look at him?' he protested. 'At Simon's son?'

Ashley gave a silent primal scream. After ricocheting from one emotional moment to another today, she was now face to face with possible disaster. Her fingers spread wider over the top of Thomas's curly head, shielding him from view. Could she claim that he needed changing? Should she concoct some story about him having a violently contagious disease? But there was no time to concoct any story for, uncomfortable in her grasp, the toddler gave a sudden squirm, wriggled and popped up to peer over her shoulder.

Vitor grinned at the infant Jack-in-the-box. 'Hello,' he said.

As the child subjected him to a solemn, no-nonsense appraisal, Ashley's heart began to hammer behind her ribs. At the same time that Thomas was studying Vitor, so Vitor was studying him. What was he thinking? she wondered, in alarm. Would he ——? Might he ——? And if he did ——

'He doesn't look like Simon,' Vitor said. 'His colouring is darker.'

'Yes.' She squeezed out a laugh. 'My mother swears he's the image of my brother when he was that age.'

'What's he called?'

'Thomas.'

'Hello, Thomas,' Vitor said, saying the name with the 's' pronounced 'sh' in the Portuguese way.

The toddler continued his unsmiling judgement.

'He's going through a shy stage,' Ashley explained, on a breath, 'and he's especially wary of men. There's a Danish guy I do business with and although Thomas knows him well, and loves going in his van, he refuses to have anything to do with Leif himself. Oh!' she exclaimed, her claim turned upside-down as the little boy abruptly launched himself from her arms and headfirst into Vitor's.

''Lo,' Thomas said, smiling up at him.

'What've you got in your hand?' Vitor asked. 'The first vehicle I ever owned was a moke like that,' he said, when the toddler's fist opened. 'When I took it to the beach it went brrmm, brrmm, up and down the sandhills.'

Thomas chuckled. 'Brrmm, brrmm,' he echoed.

Ashley looked at her son in astonishment. Vitor's pretend engine sound had been a throaty, very Portuguese purr, and he had reproduced it exactly. Her eyes drank in the cameo of the small child held by the tall man. They seemed so *easy* together. As he ran his moke up and down Vitor's shoulder, Thomas's grin said he was delighted to have met him, while Vitor gave every impression of being well used to handling a child. A thought hit her between the eyes. Perhaps he was. Although, two years ago, Vitor had shared his life with Celeste, a willowy model, somehow she had never imagined they would marry. But why not? she wondered now. They might also have started a family. Ashley's brow puckered. She knew it made no sense, but the idea of Vitor being married and having children was oddly discomfiting. Though it would be better for her if he was married, she decided. Much better.

'Juice,' Thomas demanded, suddenly remembering he was thirsty.

'Juice—what?' she enquired.

The little boy grinned. 'Juice, pease.'

'Do you think that if I said please very nicely like that your *mãe* might give me a drink, too?' Vitor said to the child in his arms. 'She may be itching for me to leave, but what with the heat and having to fight his corner——' he cast her a droll look '—this weary traveller is on the point of dehydration.'

Ashley sighed. Although the first hurdle had been

passed, she was still anxious for him to go. But refusing a drink would be churlish.

'What would the weary traveller like?' she enquired. 'Orange, home-made lemonade or a glass of lager?'

'I could murder a lager.'

'It's this way,' Ashley said, and led him into the house.

'Down,' Thomas demanded, when they reached the kitchen.

'What do you say?' Vitor enquired.

The child shone a wide smile. 'Pease.'

'There you go,' he said, and stood him on the floor.

In what Ashley considered to be a shameless playing to his audience, the little boy bestowed another wide smile.

'Tank you,' he said, being unusually polite, and toddled off to rummage in his toy box which sat in the corner.

'You said you'd made the house comfortable,' Vitor remarked, looking around, 'but you've also made it—what's the English phrase?—a joy to behold.'

Although Leif was continually pressing to be allowed to update her kitchen free of charge, Ashley had refused. After much scrubbing of the old pine units and refectory table, the bleached wood made an attractive contrast with the corn-white of the matt-finished walls. Add rush matting, yellow and white gingham curtains, and watercolours of fruit and vegetables which she had done herself, and the kitchen was rustically cosy. Her gaze followed Vitor's through the archway into the living-room. This she had painted in a warm red tone, which complemented the dark wood and brass handles of her grandfather's furniture. Rugs in jewel shades of emerald and topaz were thrown over the terracotta-tiled floor and the curtains, like the sofa and arm-chair covers, she had sewn from a heavy cream fabric. Coloured candles stood tall, there were glass boxes of shells which she and Thomas had collected, and in the stone hearth sat a vast earthenware urn filled with wild flowers. Ashley smiled. Although everything had been done on a shoestring, she was pleased with the result — and could not help feeling pleased with his praise.

'I was aiming for a Mediterranean feel,' she explained, filling a plastic mug with orange juice and taking it over to Thomas.

'And you managed it. Your artistic eye obviously extends to home-making.' Vitor accepted the brim-ming tankard which she had poured and swallowed down several eager mouthfuls. 'Nectar,' he enthused, wiping froth from his mouth with the back of his hand. He took another swig. 'What made you decide to move to Portugal?' he enquired, resting a lean hip against the table.

'This house,' Ashley said promptly.

'But you could have sold it and used the money to buy a property back home. Going to live in another country is a pretty big step to take,' he said. 'Apart from other considerations, like leaving behind all your friends and a society you'd grown up in, didn't your parents object to you taking their grandson away?'

She added ice cubes to a glass of lemonade. 'No, because they're not in England right now, either. My father works for an oil company and last summer he was seconded to their Texas headquarters for five years. Both he and my mother were keen for Thomas and me to go and live with them there, but I preferred to be independent. So here I am. And my brother, who's a trainee diplomat, is doing a stint in Brussels, so he's abroad, too,' she tacked on, for good measure.

'Wouldn't it have been simpler for you to be independent back home?' Vitor enquired.

'No,' Ashley said, beginning to feel flustered by what seemed to be shaping up into another interrogation. 'I decided that, somewhere among the pottery and handicrafts which are sold on the Algarve, there had to be an opportunity for me to utilise my design skills and earn money without the need to park Thomas with a minder. My tile painting has accomplished that. Also, the cost of living's cheaper here so the money goes further.'

'There are English holiday areas where you could have marketed your tiles,' Vitor said, plainly dubious of her argument. He took another mouthful from his glass. 'And deciding to switch to another country, especially one where the language is different, is——'

'As you may recall, I already had a fair grasp of Portuguese, so all it needed was a crash course and a month or two here to make me fluent,' Ashley said, wishing he was not so persistent. 'Now I feel entirely at home in the language.'

'Are you intending to stay long-term?'

'I'm staying until my folks return from the States. After that I don't know, but it's possible.'

'So Thomas could grow up in Portugal?'

She bobbed her head. 'The climate makes this a good place in which to bring up a child. He's yet to suffer a single cold and——'

'I get the message,' Vitor cut in. 'Life here is a seamless cloud of perfection.'

Ashley frowned. Had she been stating her case *too* forcibly? But there was no way she could divulge the pivotal reason for her deciding to move here.

'When I read somewhere that Simon Cooper's girlfriend had given birth to a son, I have to admit I was surprised,' Vitor said, with a glance at Thomas, who was engrossed in an item-by-item search of his toy box.

Her spine stiffened. 'You thought I would have had an abortion?'

'It did occur to me.'

'Because there was no man on the scene, you decided I wouldn't bother to keep the child which was growing inside of me?' Ashley demanded, her voice icy and offended.

Other people had made similar remarks. Yet, while the pregnancy might have been unplanned and she was destined to be a single parent, termination had never once been considered.

'It wasn't a matter of not bothering,' Vitor said. 'It was more——'

'Brrmm,' Thomas said, coming up to tug at his trouser leg. The little boy's search had been successful, for now he brandished the scarlet sports car which was the prize of his collection. 'Brrmm, brrmm.'

Vitor went down on his hunkers and, much to the child's glee, spent a minute or two admiring the toy.

'Thanks for the drink,' he said, rising. He arched a laconic brow. 'I hate to break your heart, but it's time I was on my way.'

'What a shame,' Ashley said demurely and, lifting Thomas on to her hip, she accompanied her visitor out of the house and down the drive.

'Mo' car!' the little boy cried joyfully, when he saw the BMW.

'When I tell my mother about Thomas she'll leap on to her hobby horse,' Vitor said drily, as he opened the car door.

'Which is?'

'How I'm thirty-eight and that if I don't find myself a wife soon she'll be too old to enjoy her grandchildren.'

So he had not married Celeste, Ashley thought. He had not married anyone.

'How is your mother?' she enquired.

'Fit and well.' Vitor climbed behind the wheel. 'She'll be delighted to know we've come across each other,' he said, speaking through the open window. 'She still has a soft spot for you.'

Ashley smiled. 'And vice versa.' When she had met Margrida d'Arcos, Vitor's widowed mother, it had been instant rapport. And in the course of a few hours the softly spoken, silver-haired woman had made her feel as though they had always been friends. 'Please remember me to her.'

'I will. I'll also get that confirmation letter off to you as quickly as possible. I'd be grateful if you'd think about my offer seriously and——' dark brown eyes snared hers '——remember that nothing less than winning ever did satisfy me.' Vitor raised a hand. '*Adeus.*'

As Ashley went back indoors, she sighed. Should she do a U-turn and sell him the house? she wondered. Her acquiescence would have one pertinent effect; it would curtail any further visits. And if his visits were not curtailed there had to be a risk that, when Vitor saw Thomas a second time, or a third, or a fourth, he would recognise the resemblance, add up dates, and realise that his mother did have a grandchild! Her eyes grew troubled. But she should not leave Vitor to recognise the resemblance, she ought to *tell* him. And she would, she promised herself—some time.

When Thomas was contentedly playing with his cars, Ashley sat down at the kitchen table. Frowning, she let her mind drift back to the events of two years ago. The catalyst for everything which had happened had been Simon, she brooded. Slim, boyish, damaged Simon. . .

CHAPTER THREE

'I'D PREFER it if you didn't tell anyone at the circuit how we come to know each other,' Simon said, his grey eyes trained on the road ahead. 'If you should be asked, just say our families are friends.'

Ashley cast a rueful glance at her escort and sighed. Although she understood why he wanted her to bend the truth, it still went against the grain.

'You expect me to lie?' she demurred.

'It's only a small one.' He slid her a coaxing smile. 'Please, Ashley.'

It was a crisp Saturday morning in February, and the young man had picked her up from her flat and was driving them to a motor-racing track in the heart of Surrey. After serving an apprenticeship in Formula Three, he had recently been signed up as second driver by Dalgety, a leading Formula One team. It was a highly coveted position and, thrilled with it and with himself, he had suggested Ashley should accompany him to a test day.

'But——' she began.

'I don't want anyone to know,' Simon said stubbornly, pushing a cowlick of pony-brown hair back from his brow.

Ashley gave in. 'Our families are friends,' she recited obediently.

He grinned. 'I felt sure you'd see it my way. I'm

going to become famous, you know, and rich,' the young man continued, with a sideways glance to check her reaction. 'In a year or two, I'll replace Vitor as Dalgety's number-one driver, then I shall move on to one of the other teams. For a vast fee, of course.'

'Aren't you being a bit——' Ashley toyed with 'big-headed' and 'absurd' '—optimistic?' she settled on. 'According to an article I read, Vitor d'Arcos is one of the finest drivers ever to grace a circuit. He's won umpteen Grands Prix and if Dalgety could have managed a tighter mechanical edge last season the general consensus is that he would have been world champion. In fact, if he weren't so loyal to Dalgety and allowed himself to be poached, he could probably have been champion several times over.'

'Vitor is good,' the young man conceded, somewhat grudgingly. He threw out his chest. 'But I'll out-perform him *and* I'll reach the top far quicker.'

Ashley gave him an old-fashioned look. Although, at twenty-five, her escort was only two years her junior, it often seemed like ten. In an attempt to impress, he would resort to extravagant gestures or issue bombastic claims—though these were restricted to his close circle of intimates.

'And the reason the boy wonder suddenly rang and invited me to watch him go through his paces was because he wanted to show off something rotten,' she teased, intent on bringing him back down to earth.

'I invited you because your mother told me that you'd realised there were more things in life than work — at long last,' Simon said pithily, 'and were in the market for some socialising.'

Ashley gave a rueful smile. 'True,' she acknowledged, 'and I'm looking forward to my first experience of Formula One.'

When she had been at college she had socialised in plenty and had had her fair share of boyfriends, Ashley reflected, as they drove along, but since then her energies had been single-mindedly channelled into her career. Since then she had deliberately avoided any involvement in man-woman affairs, so had not been held close in strong arms, not been kissed, had not made love. For a long time she had been unaware of anything lacking, but recently she had started feeling somehow. . .adrift. Ashley frowned. This did not mean she was prepared to throw herself headlong into a relationship with the first half-decent male who happened by. No, thanks, she was not *that* adrift — nor that reckless. It was simply a case of striking a better balance between work and play, and taking more of an interest in the social side of life.

'It's a shame Vitor's girlfriend, Celeste, won't be at the track today because then you could have sat with her,' Simon remarked. 'She's a friendly type and stunning-looking.' He glanced sideways, his gaze travelling from her honey-blonde head and down the violet cashmere serape which topped a black turtle-neck sweater and pencil-slim leggings. 'Though not as stunning as you.'

Ashley dug him playfully in the ribs. 'Said the gallant Sir Galahad.'

'I mean it,' he protested, sounding peeved. 'When we arrive I'll find you a seat in the stand which is reserved for guests and then return to collect you at one for lunch. I'm told the restaurant there is good.'

Three hours later, Ashley stared down at the track. All morning she had been watching low-slung, sharp-nosed cars complete several circuits, then draw into the pits to be set upon by swarms of mechanics and subjected to intensive fine-tuning. Not all the machines belonged to Dalgety. Hiring the track came expensive and so, Simon had explained, other teams were present today. She frowned at her watch. While the speed of the vehicles, the roaring surge of their engines, the *colour* of Formula One possessed an undeniable thrill, all that interested her right now was lunch. One o'clock had been and gone, and it was approaching two. Other drivers had taken a break and carried off a number of her fellow spectators, but Simon had yet to appear. Where was he? Identifying him from among the helmeted figures strapped into the cars had proved impossible. As her tummy rumbled, Ashley got to her feet. There had been a snack-dispensing machine in the entrance to the stand, so she would go and buy some chocolate.

Ashley went down one flight of stairs and another. On reaching a landing, she dithered. Which way now, left or right? She chose left, descended a further long flight and found herself facing a closed door marked 'Fire Exit'.

'Damn,' she muttered.

Pushing at the bar, Ashley looked out. The door,

which was mid-centre of the back of the stand,
opened into a protectively fenced-off area where a
number of gleaming motorhomes had been parked.
Taking a step forward, she saw that by crossing to
the side of the compound and climbing the fence she
would be able to get back round to the entrance.
Ashley dithered. There was no one in sight, but
should she trespass into what was blatantly a private
area or would she do better to tramp all the way up
the stairs again? The choice was taken from her
when a gust of wind suddenly snatched the door
from her fingers and slammed it tight shut.

The fringed ends of her serape flying behind her,
Ashley set briskly off past the motorhomes. On
reaching the three-bar fence, she clasped the top rail
and mounted the middle one. She was about to raise
a leather-booted leg when a voice suddenly shouted
behind her.

'Hey!'

Startled, she glanced back to find a man clad in
the scarlet overalls and white crash helmet of a
driver standing a few yards away. Ashley wobbled
and clung on. It was not Simon; this individual was
too tall and more broadly built. The man walked
forward. Was he about to bark out a reprimand? she
wondered. Haul her off to the stewards? Or make
some patronising remark about her cute rear end
and how he would be delighted to give her a lift
over? Ashley groaned inwardly. Thanks to her
looks, blonde hair and figure, being chatted up by
lascivious males was an ongoing nuisance.

The mask of helmet and balaclava beneath meant

that all she could see were the man's eyes and mouth — but his eyes shone a lustrous dark brown and his lips were fine sculpted. As his gaze tangled with hers, Ashley felt a tug of emotional recognition. A sharp tug. A mutual tug. How could that be, she wondered, when they had never met before? As if he, too, was perplexed, the man frowned, then he lifted off his helmet and peeled away the balaclava. Her heart stopped beating. His hair was dark and rumpled, his face clean-shaven, his skin a sultry gold.

'Your wrap's caught on a nail,' he warned, in a voice with the kind of husky foreign accent which, should he decide to recite the phone book, would still be entirely enchanting.

Ashley looked down and freed it. 'Thanks,' she said.

Climbing from the fence, she turned to face him. All they had done was look at each other and exchange a few very prosaic words, yet something magical was happening. Something she could not begin to understand, but something which made her want to know more, much more, about this wonderful stranger.

'I realise this area is reserved for racing personnel,' Ashley said, wondering if her heart was ever going to start beating again, 'and I'm sorry to trespass. But I came out of the stand through the fire exit and I can't get back in. So I thought that if I climbed the fence I'd be able to reach the entrance and the machine where I can buy some chocolate. Simon was supposed to take me for lunch an hour ago,' she said, hearing herself rattle on, yet unable to stop, 'but he seems to have forgotten and I'm hungry and——'

'You must be Ashley. Simon told me you were coming today,' the wonderful stranger said, and, clasping his helmet to his chest, he held out a hand. 'I'm Vitor d'Arcos.'

'Pleased to meet you,' Ashley said.

Although his handshake was firm and his smile warm, she recognised a subtle change. The tug which had linked and drawn them together had gone. Her heart lurched into rhythm behind her ribcage. Yet had it ever existed? Had there been magic—or was it just an illusion? Ashley drew the soft wool of her serape closer around her neck. Perhaps it was due to her feeling adrift, but she appeared to have suffered a brainstorm. That mutual tug had not existed. When he had looked at her so intently, Vitor d'Arcos had been curious about an intruder, that was all.

'I've just left Simon poring over computer print-outs with an engineer, so you're right, he has forgotten about you,' he told her, and paused. 'I'm glad to say.'

'Why glad?' Ashley protested.

'Because one of the most important qualities a driver must have is concentration. If you're travelling at two hundred miles an hour and your mind wanders for even a fraction of a second, it can be fatal. I'm going to have lunch,' Vitor continued, 'so, as Simon's otherwise engaged, how about joining me?'

She smiled. 'Thank you.'

'I need to go and change,' he said, with a gesture towards one of the motorhomes, 'but I won't be long.'

True to his word, Vitor d'Arcos quickly returned, this time wearing a cream thick-knit sweater, blue jeans and a black leather jacket. On their way over to the restaurant, several people greeted him and, once inside the low-ceilinged room, more stopped him to chat. All made their admiration plain, yet he showed no airs. Simon, take note, Ashley thought.

'You realise the rumour-mill will have already marked us down as lovers?' Vitor enquired, as they joined a few stragglers beside the buffet table.

Her heart performed a loop-the-loop.

'L-lovers?' Ashley said.

'Celeste may attend every Grand Prix, but——' his dark brown eyes met hers '—that won't stop the gossips assuming that the next place we're heading is into bed.'

A myriad images—all of them disturbing—flashed through her head. Vitor d'Arcos was in excellent physical shape and, with his mature self-assurance, would doubtless be a demon lover.

'You like your girlfriend to be with you at every Grand Prix?' Ashley enquired, making a studious inspection of the array of roasts, quiches and salads.

'Celeste likes to be at every Grand Prix,' he responded. 'Personally, I'd rather she showed more interest in her career.'

'Which is?'

'Modelling. Celeste's capable of reaching the top, if she set her mind to it. As you have.'

'You know what I do?' Ashley asked, in surprise.

'I know all about you.' Vitor helped himself to a slice of gammon. 'Simon's filled me in in glorious detail.'

'Oh.' She was not sure what that meant. 'It isn't every man who approves of women having ambition,' Ashley remarked a touch cryptically — for when she had been made a director several of her male colleagues had found it very hard to handle.

'Why shouldn't I approve?' he enquired, when they had filled their plates and found a table. 'I'm ambitious.'

'Even so, it surprises me.' She gave a mischievous grin. 'Especially as you're Portuguese and most of the Portuguese men I've met have held macho, conservative views on a woman's role in life.'

Vitor arched an amused brow. 'You have a vast experience of my fellow countrymen?' he enquired.

Ashley laughed. 'No, but until my late teens I spent each and every holiday on the Algarve so I have had conversations with quite a few.'

'You spoke to them in Portuguese?'

'*Sim.*'

'You still speak it?'

'*Sim,*' she said again, 'though I'm a bit rusty.'

Vitor switched to his native tongue. 'Would you like some practice?' he asked.

Ashley nodded. She had a natural flair for languages and it would be fun to brush up a little.

'*Sim, por favor,*' she told him.

They talked for ages, making each other laugh, finding shared points of view, generally having a good time — until Vitor realised he was overdue back at the track.

Ashley gazed out of the car window at the country-side which was bathed in September sunshine. In another few minutes, she and Simon would be arriving at the Sintra home of Margrida d'Arcos and she would be meeting Vitor again. Since February when they had chatted in Portuguese, she had seen the racing driver just twice. Once, a fortnight later, when Simon had invited her to another test day, and then in July at the British Grand Prix. Both meetings had taken place in the company of others and been brief.

Yet, as the months had rolled on, she had not forgotten him. On the contrary, time and again Ashley had found herself thinking about Vitor's looks, that purring accent, those first moments when they had first met. And ever since Simon had revealed that he had accepted the lunch invitation her adrenalin had been humming. She grimaced. She was acting like some idiotic schoolgirl, not an intelligent woman, she thought in exasperation. Vitor might find her easy to talk to, but he had no other interest in her. Why should he when he shared his life with a girl who, with clouds of dark hair, olive skin and a slender figure, was just as stunning as Simon had claimed? And ultra-devoted. Yester-day, when she and Celeste had watched the

Portuguese Grand Prix together, the model had done nothing but drool.

'I adore Vitor in his driver's overalls,' she had declared, giggling. 'It's said that if the flame-retardant with which they're treated could be bottled it'd be the first guaranteed aphrodisiac.' As she gazed down at where his car waited in pole position, Celeste's giggles had changed into a pout. 'I wish Vitor didn't have this bee in the bonnet about me being a working girl. I was all set to attend his mother's barbecue, but then he discovered I had an assignment and refused to let me cancel.'

Ashley now tugged at the belt which cinched the waist of her amber-coloured silk shift dress. The closer she came to meeting Vitor d'Arcos again, the more her adrenalin surged and the more she wished there had been something to prevent *her* attendance.

'The hills of Sintra mean that even in the height of summer the town has a freshness, which is why the rich people used to build their country houses here to escape the heat of Lisbon,' Ashley said, resolutely switching her thoughts away from her host and to a guide book which she had been reading. She looked out at the lush green wooded hillsides which rose up ahead. 'Royalty also built their palaces here,' she continued, and indicated two large conical chimneys which towered above the trees. 'That must be the Paco da Vila or National Palace.'

Simon was not listening. 'Sixth place,' he said, with a triumphant hoot. 'I came sixth and gained my first championship point!'

'Captain Fantastic did very well,' she agreed, her

tone a little weary because the young man had not only spent every minute of the previous evening blowing his own trumpet, but much of their journey today, too.

'I did bloody marvellous! Shows what a boost it was having you here.' He slid a sideways glance. 'Maybe if you'd accepted my offer of an air ticket to all the other Grands Prix I would have come in the first six there, too.'

'It wasn't possible for me to take time off work,' Ashley protested.

Nor did I have the inclination, she added silently. For me, a little bit of race watching goes a long way. Though, that apart, she regarded the offer as a typically Simon over-the-top gesture, and felt sure that, had she said she would journey to Mexico or Hungary or wherever, the free travel would have been abruptly rescinded. It was only because his repeated invitations had made her think that maybe the young man *did* need the support of someone familiar that she had agreed to come to Lisbon — and because, after a hardworking summer, she had been in need of a break. But the long weekend was on the strict understanding that she pay her own way.

'Vitor came third and would have been first if his car hadn't hit fuel problems on the final lap,' Simon continued, his mind fixed on the race. His fingers tightened around the steering-wheel, their knuckles draining white. 'But I'll beat the bastard before the season's over.'

At this vow, which he had repeated to her so often

it was beginning to sound like a mantra, Ashley frowned. Few people realised it, but beneath Simon's confident and charming exterior lurked a mass of insecurities. These meant he took everything personally and, instead of meeting a challenge purely as a challenge, he became aggressive about proving that *he*, Simon Cooper, was top dog. It was the combination of this aggression with his talent which had brought him so far, and yet while Vitor possessed a professional's dedication to winning Simon had plainly identified his team-mate as a bitter rival who must be trounced at all costs.

'You're not involved in a vendetta,' Ashley protested.

The young man stared straight ahead. 'Where now?' he asked, for they were approaching a junction.

'Left,' she said, inspecting the map on her knee. 'Then it's left again at the next crossroads and we're there.'

The d'Arcos family home was a nineteenth-century villa of elegant proportions, with a weathered red-tile roof and long upper balcony. Surrounded by lemon trees and fragrant bushes of wild lavender, it sat above the town which Lord Byron had once described as 'a glorious Eden'. As they parked and headed for the open front door, a smiling woman in a dusky pink two-piece and with her silver hair caught back in a chignon appeared to welcome them.

'I'm Margrida d'Arcos,' she said, ushering them inside. 'And you are?'

'Simon Cooper,' Simon promptly declared, and looked expectant.

'Ah, you're the clever fellow who took sixth place yesterday,' their hostess said obligingly. 'I watched on television and you drove a fine race. Many congratulations.'

The young man beamed. 'Thank you. It was——'

'And my name's Ashley Fleming,' Ashley said, fearful that Simon might start patting himself on the back yet again.

Margrida shook her hand and graciously accepted the flowers which she had brought.

'I understand you speak Portuguese like a native,' she said, with a smile.

Ashley grinned. 'I wish I did, but——'

'But you try,' said a well-modulated voice, and she turned to see Vitor coming along the Persian carpeted hall.

He wore a short-sleeved white shirt which was open at the collar and classic button-fly jeans. As always, he gave off an impression of coiled masculine energy and, as it always did whenever she saw him, Ashley's heartbeat quickened.

'Your trouble with the fuel was bad luck yesterday,' she commiserated, after greetings had been exchanged.

'At the time I wanted to weep or murder somebody, but now——' he shrugged pragmatic shoulders '—all I can do is wait for the next time.' He grinned at Simon. 'And hope my up-and-coming team-mate here hasn't decided to annihilate me and grab all the glory for himself.'

'I have,' the young man told him, and, although he smiled, Ashley knew he was in deadly earnest. 'Unfortunately we have to leave at three,' Simon continued. 'The mechanics are stripping down my engine and I need to be there.'

'Leave at three?' Margrida d'Arcos protested, in dismay. She turned to Ashley. 'Surely you don't both need to go then? If I arrange a lift, couldn't you travel back to Lisbon later?'

Ashley hesitated. While the less time she spent in Vitor's proximity, the less wear and tear there would be on her nerves, his mother's appeal made insisting on an early exit seem impolite.

'I could. Thank you,' she said.

Their hostess smiled. 'Come and join the others.'

After every Portuguese Grand Prix, so Simon had explained, Senhora d'Arcos invited the Dalgety personnel and their partners to lunch. Now, leading the way across a parquet-floored drawing-room, she took them out through French windows into a large walled garden. Here, on a sun-dappled terrace shaded by tall eucalyptus trees, about forty chattering and laughing guests were gathered.

After asking what they would like to drink, Vitor provided cut-crystal glasses of *vinho verde*, but his duties as host quickly took him away to pour refills and greet other arrivals.

'Have you visited Sintra before?' Margrida enquired.

Ashley shook her head. 'Never, but I've been reading up on the history.'

'Have you read about King João and his flirtation?' her hostess asked.

She grinned, intrigued. 'No, please tell me.'

'The story goes that the king was caught kissing one of the ladies-in-waiting of his English queen, Philippa of Lancaster. He swore the kiss was *por bem*, which in translation means——' Margrida thought for a moment '—"without consequence" or "of no consequence", and his wife believed him.'

Simon had been growing restless, but all of a sudden he spotted someone with whom he could discuss yesterday's success.

'Excuse me,' he said, and hurried off.

'However,' Margrida continued, 'the incident created so much gossip among his courtiers that King João became annoyed and he ordered a ceiling in the palace to be painted with as many magpies as there were chattering ladies. Every bird is different. Each carries the red rose of Lancaster in its claw and, beside its beak, the words "*por bem*", which are intended to signify the king's blamelessness down through the ages. You should visit the Paco da Vila and see the Magpie Room.'

'I'd like to, but my flight leaves first thing in the morning,' Ashley said regretfully.

'Then you must come to Sintra next spring and stay with me, and we shall go together,' her hostess declared, in a sincere statement of intent.

Ashley's gaze went to Vitor, who was talking to guests. While she felt sure she would enjoy his mother's company, she was reluctant to encourage an association which could involve further contact with him. She sipped from her glass. Exactly *why* she should be so wary of further contact she did not know, but avoiding it seemed prudent.

'If I can get the time off work,' she murmured, being carefully non-committal.

All of a sudden, the activities of a chef who was arranging steaks and kebabs on a barbecue further down the garden caught Margrida's attention.

'I must go, my dear. While he's capable, he does have a tendency to overcook.' She smiled. 'But I'm sure that after being monopolised by me for so long you'll be anxious to return to your boyfriend.'

'Hmm,' Ashley said, being non-committal again.

As if on cue, Simon appeared, and not much later their hostess announced that lunch was ready. After the barbecue, which was accompanied by salad and jacket potatoes, came a sticky almond cake dessert, followed by a selection of local cheeses and fresh fruit. As Ashley poured herself a second cup of rich dark coffee at a side-table, she frowned again. Not only had Margrida assumed that Simon was her boyfriend, but Celeste had clearly thought the same yesterday—and just now a hearty, middle-aged Dalgety executive had stopped her to say how fortunate their new driver was to have such a pretty and successful young lady as his *amor*. She sat the cafetière firmly back down on its stand. The matter must be rectified.

Ashley waited until their fellow diners had drifted away to explore the gardens or dip their hands in the cool water which tinkled in the stone fountains, and then moved her chair closer to her escort's.

'I may have agreed to keep quiet about how we know each other, but I didn't agree to our relationship being viewed as an affair!' she protested. 'I've no idea what you've been saying, but the general impression here——'

'I haven't said anything,' Simon cut in, two spots of colour blooming on his cheeks. 'I mean, it's obvious people will jump to that conclusion.'

'Is it? I only appear on infrequent occasions, so why don't they think I'm just a family friend?' Ashley demanded.

He looked sulky. 'What's wrong with being regarded as my girl?'

'Nothing, except that I'm not. If people know we met because my parents fostered you when you were a teenager, they aren't going to think any the less of you,' she said, her voice gentle because this was an old hang-up, one which her family had spent years trying to dispel. 'On the contrary, they'll be full of admiration at the success you're making of your life.'

'Look,' Simon said impatiently, 'so far there have only been passing mentions of me in the papers, but when I become famous the media interest will soar. And if it's discovered that I spent most of my childhood in care, then reporters could make enquiries and turn it into a big thing.'

Ashley sighed. While she felt he should be honest with his colleagues, she could understand a reluctance to have stories about how his ne'er-do-well father had walked out before his birth and he had subsequently been neglected by his mother appear in the Press.

'All right, I won't say anything. But,' she added pungently, 'I'd be obliged if you'd make it clear to your Formula One buddies that you and I are just good friends!'

'Will do,' her foster brother agreed.

'You've never had any trouble attracting the opposite sex, so how come you don't have anyone in tow now?' Ashley enquired. 'Hordes of girls hang around the racetracks and——'

'They're all airheads,' Simon said witheringly, and checked his watch. It was three o'clock. 'I could be tied up until quite late,' he told her, 'but as soon as I'm free I'll come round to your hotel.'

She shook her head. 'There's no point. I have to be at the airport before six tomorrow, so I'm going to bed early.'

'When will I see you again?' the young man asked. 'There are only two more Grands Prix to be held this season, one in——'

'Sorry, I'm tied up for the next couple of months with long-haul business trips,' Ashley interrupted. 'I'll catch up with you some time when you're back in England.'

After he had gone, she chatted with several of the other guests, learned more local history from Margrida, got pinned down again by the Dalgety executive. Her path failed to cross with Vitor's, yet throughout the afternoon Ashley remained constantly aware of him. Of how his hands would move through the air when he was making a point. Of the dark curls which showed in the neck of his shirt. Of his neat backside in his jeans. This awareness irritated. She was not in the habit of ogling men, and although, over the past few months, she had accepted a few invitations to dinner or the theatre, none of her dates had even remotely *magnetised*.

In time, people began to leave. Ashley waited to be told which of them she was to accompany, but the numbers dwindled and nothing was said.

'Vitor's driving you back,' Margrida informed her, as the last group of guests bade their host goodbye.

Her heart tripped. 'He is?'

'I am?' Vitor enquired, overhearing and swinging round in surprise. 'I didn't know that.'

'Ashley's hotel is in a different part of town from where everyone else is staying and it seemed unfair to expect them to take a detour,' his mother explained. 'And you are going back to your apartment.'

Ashley frowned. As well as surprise, she had heard irritation tamped down in Vitor's voice. Well, she was not exactly overjoyed to have him acting as her chauffeur, either!

'I could ring for a taxi,' she suggested, when the final guests had departed and she was standing with her host and hostess on the drive.

Margrida would not hear of it. 'Vitor's happy to take you,' she declared serenely, and kissed her on both cheeks. 'It's been such a pleasure meeting you and don't forget what I said about the spring.'

'I won't,' Ashley said, with a weak smile.

'Instead of going straight back, why not drive up into the hills and show Ashley the view?' Margrida suggested, as Vitor ushered her into a four-wheel-drive Suzuki.

He gave a terse nod and switched on the ignition. With a squeal of tyres, the dark green vehicle shot away down the drive.

'I'm sorry you've been lumbered with running me back,' Ashley said crisply, as they turned on to the road. 'However, there's no need to bother showing me the view.'

Vitor rammed the gear stick into third. 'It's no bother.'

'Liar,' she said.

He shot her a look. 'I told my mother I'd take you and I will,' he declared, his tone aiming for civility, yet laced with impatience.

Ashley brushed strands of pale honey-coloured hair from her shoulders. 'Your choice.'

He drove along the road for two or three miles, then turned off on to a stone-walled lane which led up a forested hillside. Higher the Suzuki climbed, and higher, until the lane petered out into a dirt track and gradually the trees became fewer. Over one last rise, and they were driving across a grassy boulder-strewn plateau which seemed to be on the top of the world.

'It's years since I've been up here,' Vitor said, 'but if I remember correctly there's a good vantage point another mile on.'

All of a sudden, the four-wheel-drive gave a cough and a splutter.

'Is something the matter?' Ashley enquired, as he peered down at the instrument panel.

The vehicle slowed and came to a halt.

Vitor turned to her. 'We've run out of gas,' he said.

Dismay vied with annoyance. She had wanted to get back to her hotel and away from him but, first, he had insisted on driving her out into the wilderness, and now he had marooned them.

'That's twice in two days you've had fuel problems,' Ashley observed.

Vitor picked up the tightness in her voice. 'You think I made this happen on purpose?' he demanded.

'No.' She bestowed an on-and-off smile. 'But I do think that, for most people, ensuring your vehicle has sufficient petrol before you embark on a journey is a sensible precaution.'

A muscle clenched in his jaw. 'During the Formula One season, I devote ninety per cent of my energy, thoughts, awareness — of *me* — to racing,' he rasped, 'and the other ten per cent to my building company. Which means, if you'd care to do a simple sum——'

'You have a building company?' Ashley cut in.

'I do. I came to motor sport after I'd qualified as an architect and gained a business degree,' he told her curtly.

'You qualified in Lisbon?'

'I studied architecture here, but then went to the States for the degree,' Vitor replied, and rapped out brief details. 'So, with all my thoughts channelled of necessity elsewhere,' he continued, 'is it so surprising if something like the position of a needle on a petrol gauge does occasionally escape my attention?'

Ashley stared ahead. 'Where's the nearest garage?' she enquired.

'Down the other side of the hill and roughly a couple of miles on.'

She opened her door and jumped out. 'Let's go.'

'You intend to come with me?' Vitor said, climbing out to frown at her across the bonnet.

'It seems preferable to sitting here for goodness knows how long twiddling my thumbs.'

'You could spoil your sandals,' he warned.

Raising a foot, Ashley eyed the network of fine straps and the spindly heel. 'I'll take my chance.'

Vitor frowned up at the scattering of cloud which had appeared in the clear blue sky. 'It might rain and then your hair would get wet.'

He was confusing her with Celeste, she thought impatiently. Yesterday, as they had chatted, the model had been continually fussing with her mane of black curls, or admiring her long finger nails, or smoothing down the skirt of her grey suede suit.

'At which point I'd have hysterics and writhe on the ground?' Ashley enquired. 'If it should rain, it's not going to be for a very long time.'

They had been walking for less than ten minutes when it began to spit.

'Would you like to turn back?' Vitor enquired.

It had only taken a matter of yards for her to acknowledge that her sandals made abysmal hiking boots. Every so often she would totter, and since her companion walked more purposefully she was having to add a half-step every so often in order to keep up. Yet as he had committed himself to bringing her up here, so Ashley felt stubbornly committed to walking.

'No, thanks,' she replied.

They trekked on, and the rain became heavier.

'Weather forecasting doesn't appear to be your forte,' Vitor remarked, eyeing the wet spots which were beginning to dot his shirt.

Ashley looked up at a grey ball of a cloud which hung directly overhead. 'It's only a passing shower,' she declared.

He thrust her a diminishing glance. 'Perhaps, but while getting soaked to the skin may put a kick into your day it does not appeal to me.' He pointed. 'There used to be a barn in that dip over to the left. I suggest we go and shelter.'

Ashley followed the direction of his finger. Vitor had not 'suggested'. He had issued an instruction; one which the glint in his eye warned she disobeyed at her peril.

'Good idea,' she said.

Another few totters and another series of hasty hoppity-skips, and they were looking down at a ramshackle wooden building which sat in a hollow among yellow bushes of gorse.

'May I give you a hand?' her companion offered, as she took an unsteady step forward.

While she would have preferred to manage alone, Ashley did not relish slip-sliding down the slope in an undignified arm-flailing fashion, nor on her bottom.

'Please,' she said stiffly.

Linking strong fingers with hers, Vitor kept her upright as they made their way down the bank.

'Thank you,' she said, as they entered the barn, but when she attempted to withdraw her hand his grip tightened.

As Ashley glanced questioningly at him, her heart began to thump. Vitor was looking at her in the way he had looked at her so many months ago — when they had first met, when she had felt that tug. When she had *thought* she had felt a tug, her mind corrected.

'How am I supposed to resist the inevitable?' he demanded, sounding angry, and pulled at her hand, jolting her forward.

'What — what do you mean?' she said, breathless because now only inches separated them, because now the tang of his sandalwood aftershave was filling her nostrils, because now she could feel the heat coming off his body.

'Why do you think I've been avoiding you today? Why do you imagine you've been so. . .twitchy?' All of a sudden, his anger dropped away. 'The first time I saw you, I knew,' Vitor said, in a low driven voice. 'And you knew it, too. Didn't you?'

CHAPTER FOUR

ASHLEY gazed up into dark brown eyes which were sending intimate messages and telling her everything she had been longing to hear.

'Yes,' she said simply.

Raising a hand, Vitor clasped her chin in his long fingers and held her almost fiercely for a moment.

'You are a sorceress. A beautiful sorceress,' he muttered, and then he was kissing her — on her face, on her throat, in her hair, on her mouth. Kissing her urgently, passionately, hungrily.

With no hesitation her lips opened to his, and as their breath and tongues mingled Ashley strained closer. Vitor seemed to have something beneath his skin which had connected with something beneath hers, and her breathing was quickening, her pulses raced, she no longer felt as if she was standing on solid ground.

As kiss followed riotous kiss, his fingertips trailed along the smooth column of her throat and down to the silky fabric of her dress. Ashley waited, waited. Touch me, she implored silently. *Please*. When Vitor's thumb brushed across the tight pinnacles of her breasts, a heat spiralled from the base of her stomach and spread relentlessly through her body.

Vitor caressed her for a moment but then, impatient for the nakedness of the woman who had

been such an obstinate aching presence in his bloodstream, he eased the amber silk from her shoulders
and unhooked her lacy bra.

'So high, so proud,' he murmured, his dark eyes
devouring the beauty of her exposed breasts.

He lifted his hands and as they closed over the
aching swollen curves a sound female and feral
emerged from the back of her throat. Ashley's head
fell back. She arched her spine. She needed to be
caressed and he caressed her, massaging and pinch-
ing at the puckered rose-pink nipples, until the heat
burst into searing flame and wildfire licked over her
body.

'Now. . .we must. . .' Vitor muttered thickly, and
looked around.

In a corner of the barn, a pile of hay spilled in
untidy abandon. He drew her down with him on to
it. Ashley felt the prickle of the dried grass against
her back, heard the pitter-patter of rain on the roof,
gazed into the gloom, but, as Vitor lowered his dark
head, all awareness of their surroundings faded.
Now only the two of them existed. Now all that
mattered was their mutual desire. Vitor's kiss took
the whole of her erect nipple into his mouth and she
stirred, made restless by the insistent tweak of an
invisible wire which seemed to go directly from her
breasts to the pulsing nerve-cluster between her
thighs. As his tongue rasped across the sensitive
peaks, as his teeth gently bit, Ashley curled her
fingers into the dark hair on the top of his head. She
had never felt like this before, she thought dazedly.
Never. Never. Never.

Stricken by a sudden overwhelming need, her fingers flew in search of his shirt buttons. She had to undo them, had to strip the white poplin from his chest, had to touch him.

'Let me,' Vitor murmured as she pulled, and he twisted free of the garment.

Wishing she could cover all of him at once, Ashley stroked her hands across his chest. She rubbed her fingertips over the whorls of coarse dark hair, explored the contours of his muscles, caressed his golden skin. When she bent her head and traced the outline of a flat brown nipple with the tip of her tongue, Vitor groaned. For a moment or two, he withstood the pleasure, but then he took hold of her hips and drew her hard into him. Ashley trembled. She closed her eyes. The jut of his maleness against her had unleashed an erotic force which was so powerful it scared her. Gulping down a breath, she lifted her lids — and found him looking at her.

Wordlessly Vitor asked a question and wordlessly Ashley answered. There was nothing she could do to resist him, though she did not want to resist. It did not matter that it was only the fourth time they had met; she knew this moment was exceptional in her life and that, while their physical passion might be impulsive and unplanned, it was inescapable.

Vitor drew her dress from her and a pair of white bikini briefs followed, then he swiftly undressed. Sinking back down, he drew her close again. As they met, breast to chest, thighs against thighs, legs intertwined, their bodies seemed to show recognition. There was no awkwardness, no shyness, no inhibitions. Instead with every open-mouthed kiss, with every fevered touch, each lifted the other on to a higher and increasingly higher plane of ecstasy.

As Ashley's hands explored the bones of his pelvis, Vitor took a deep controlling breath.

'Hold me,' he implored, and when her fingers closed around his heated length he groaned again.

His hand moved to the triangle of fair curls between her thighs and as he caressed the glistening pink bud which was hidden there she cried out for his possession. Vitor entered her and Ashley's hips lifted, meeting the hard rhythmic thrusts which seemed to penetrate to the very depths of her womb. His rhythm quickened and she clung, her fingernails marking his back. Now everything was jet-black and fiery red. Now everything was sliding, tipping, falling. Now everything was *Vitor*, on her, in her, around her. . .and then the world erupted.

Later, Ashley stood in the doorway of the barn. She inhaled. The rain had stopped and the air was filled with the sweet smell of freshly washed earth. Smiling, she gazed around her. Wet blades of grass gleamed like so many tiny polished green spears in the early evening sunshine and the gorse bushes sparkled with diamond drops. A distant rainbow formed a delicately coloured arc. She gave a soft sigh of contentment. That the world should be so enchanting after the enchantment of Vitor's lovemaking was entirely appropriate.

Ashley tilted her head. Was that the sound of an engine, the Suzuki's engine, in the distance? Yes. As they had lain together in the glorious lethargy which followed passion, Vitor had told her he would go for the petrol, but that he would go alone. Drowsy and sated, she had not argued. He had kissed her and left, giving her ample time in which to dress, to comb her hair, to apply lipstick to lips which were softly bruised by her lover's ardour.

As the engine noise grew louder, Ashley set off across the grass. She had begun to climb the bank when the four-wheel drive suddenly appeared on the rim above, bumped down and drew to a halt alongside.

'Thanks, but I was coming up to meet you,' she said, as Vitor came round to open the passenger door.

'I didn't think your sandals would be adequate to the task,' he replied, and gestured for her to climb aboard.

He said nothing after that. In silence, Vitor restarted the engine. In silence, he drove them out of the hollow and back on to the track. He must still be basking in the afterglow of their lovemaking— and was no doubt a little shocked by its unexpectedness—Ashley thought, as the track gave way to the lane and his silence continued. He did not feel like talking. Not yet. It was understandable. But as the lane turned into the metalled road, and Vitor remained mute, she cast him a glance. His expression was grave and he looked deep in thought. Could he be thinking about his girlfriend?

This far Celeste had not crossed her mind, but now Ashley felt a sharp twinge of guilt. The model, who had been friendly towards her, was going to be hurt. Yet if she felt uncomfortable, Vitor must be feeling so much worse. She looked at him again. Was he wondering how to break it to Celeste that their relationship was over? Was he worrying about how the Portuguese girl might react? Chances were she would react badly. After all, they had been together for a couple of years and she did idolise him.

A line cut between Ashley's brows. If Vitor imagined she was going to demand an immediate showdown with the model, he was wrong. Neither would she be shouting about their liaison from the rooftops. Knowing what they shared was enough for now, and she was content for him to pick his moment, take his time and let Celeste down gently.

Ashley moistened her lips. 'About this afternoon. . .' she began.

'I can't get involved in anything right now,' Vitor said sternly. 'I'm sorry, but it's impossible.' He turned to frown. 'You understand?'

In the cruel treachery of his words she had only one thought — that she must not seem surprised.

'Yes, yes, I understand,' she assured him.

As he returned his attention to the road Ashley sat motionless, her happiness hacked to shreds. What she understood was that she had grossly misinterpreted the situation. It was not Celeste whom Vitor had been wondering how to ditch, it had been her! A bitter laugh rose up like bile in her throat. All he had 'known' when they had first met had been lust, pure and simple. For her, their lovemaking might have been an almost mystical fusing of bodies

and identities, yet for him it had been no more than
a roll in the hay. Literally. But, having only ever
slept with one other man — a fellow student back in
her college days — she could be classed as a sexual
novice, Ashley thought tormentedly, whereas Vitor
d'Arcos was an experienced man of the world. Years
of celibacy had made her highly susceptible and he,
a demon lover, had known exactly how to turn her
on. Her cheeks burned, as she recalled just how
turned-on she had been, how forward, how wanton.

For Vitor, women offering themselves up to him
must be an occupational hazard; so did he regard
her as yet one more race-track groupie? He must,
for hadn't she let him make love to her after just a
handful of meetings, when they hardly knew each
other? Her stomach twisted. She felt sick. How
could she have been so thoughtless, so foolish, done
something so unarguably *dangerous*? Ashley wondered. A bolt of pain rocketed through her skull.
Using that famed double standard which made it
acceptable for men to indulge in chance conquests,
but which castigated women, Vitor would now associate her with casual sex and loose morals. It hadn't
been like that, she wanted to howl. For me, our
passion was a devout involvement of heart, body
and mind. A devout involvement? Ashley gave a
terse silent laugh. There was only one way to
describe the afternoon's events — as a catastrophe.

As their journey continued Ashley waited for her
companion's mood to lift, but Vitor remained silent
and sombre. Why, she wondered, when she had
effectively let him off the hook? They had reached

the hilly avenues of Lisbon when it occurred to her that he could be worried about how she might behave when the time came for them to part. Would she scream insults, or perhaps cling on to him for grim death and beg for another chance? Either way, someone could recognise that the man at the receiving end of her hysteria was Vitor d'Arcos, and inform the media. Ashley tightened a pearl earring. What she would do was exit with as much style as possible, given the situation.

'About this afternoon,' she said again, as they came to a halt outside the pillared portico of her hotel. She shone a carefree smile. 'We both know that it was *por bem*.'

Vitor looked at her in confusion. '*Por bem*?' he repeated.

'You've heard the story of King João and the lady-in-waiting?'

'*Sim*. Yes,' he muttered, and frowned as though he was having difficulty getting a grip on what she was saying.

'We can put this afternoon in the "of no consequence" category, too,' Ashley declared brightly.

He opened his mouth as though he was about to say something, but then he closed it again. While he might have dismissed her, Vitor appeared to find it disconcerting that she should turn the tables and dismiss him. But, of course, it would not happen too often, she thought astringently.

'You're saying we should forget it?' he enquired.

'I already have,' Ashley declared and, climbing

from the vehicle, she swung jauntily into the hotel without looking behind her.

Like a pack of buzzing, whining, huge-tyred hornets, the racing cars zapped past on the track below. Then there was silence. Shrugging out of the bronze jacket which covered a sandwashed white silk shirt and gabardine trousers, Ashley resettled herself in her seat. TV monitors were suspended from the roof of the stand to enable spectators to follow the progress of the race around the circuit, and she raised her eyes. She sighed. Six weeks ago, she had vowed that, from now on, she would avoid the Formula One world like the plague, but fate had decided otherwise and here she was, watching the Australian Grand Prix.

On her arrival in Adelaide to discuss a joint venture with a fabric firm, she had been unaware that the last race of the season would be held here during her stay, Ashley reflected, but the newspapers had soon put her straight. Unsettled at having come halfway around the world to find herself in the same town at the same time as Vitor d'Arcos, she had skipped over any articles which mentioned him, but, on turning a page, had found an article which she could *not* ignore. Ashley's eyes drifted down from the screen and she frowned. Contrary to making it plain that they were just friends, Simon had indulged in some imaginary kiss-and-tell. 'My girlfriend, Ashley Fleming, is a busy company director,' he had told a reporter, 'which means she can't be with me at most Grands Prix. However, when we do meet up it's well worth while.' And, as if that nudge-nudge, wink-wink had not been enough, her foster brother had provided a photograph to illustrate the article which had seemed to prove his claims.

'I didn't think you'd mind,' Simon had said yesterday, when she had angrily voiced her objections.

'You didn't think I'd find out!' she had retorted.

He had smiled a coaxing smile. 'It is only a local paper.'

'But with half the world's sports Press in town, the idea that we're a twosome could be picked up by other reporters and become accepted knowledge,' Ashley had protested.

'And that's a fate worse than death?'

'No, not exactly, but——'

'You wouldn't be making such a fuss if you'd been named as Vitor's girlfriend,' the young man had declared.

Ashley's frown cut deeper. After that the conversation had gathered a startling momentum of statements, random guesses, admissions and had ended with her using her foster brother as a confidant — though now she regretted it.

She refolded her jacket. But what was she doing here today? Ashley wondered. Exactly *why* had she come? She might have extracted Simon's solemn oath that if she attended as he wished, the pretence that she was his girlfriend would be dropped for once and for all, but was that the whole reason? In truth, she found watching the endless circuiting a little tedious and especially when there was no one to talk to. Had she hoped that Simon would alert Vitor to her presence, and that he might search her out, explain he had rethought and declare undying love? Her lips formed a bleak smile. The idea belonged in the realms of fantasy. After six weeks of silence, the chances of her one-time lover rethinking were zero.

All of a sudden, she realised there had been a collective intake of breath and that everyone around her was staring at the monitors. When Ashley looked up, she saw chaos. A racing car had crashed, wrecking a safety barrier, spectacularly demolishing a wall and causing several other machines to spin and swerve. She narrowed her eyes. The air was so full of flying stones, pieces of metal, swirling dust, that it was impossible to make out the markings on the car which had ended up skewed across the track, but it looked very much like a Dalgety. Her fingers flew to her throat in distress. Could that be Simon in the cockpit. . .or Vitor?

The TV commentator was excitedly describing the drama, but although she strained to hear she could not pick out the name of the victim. Ashley had swung to a middle-aged woman beside her to demand if she knew when the camera shot changed. A driver had wrenched himself from another machine and was running back.

'Vitor d'Arcos is going to his team-mate's aid,' the commentator shouted.

So the figure who sat inert and limp was Simon, Ashley realised numbly. Reaching the car, Vitor lunged forward to release the young man and lift him free, but the chassis had twisted. Frantically, he set to work dismantling it. Vitor was tearing at jagged pieces of bodywork when a flame spurted from beneath.

'He wants to get the lad out in case the fuel explodes,' the woman beside her muttered.

The flame was rapidly joined by others, but Vitor continued to tear and pull. Ashley was frowning at the flames which had begun to dart around his feet when two other drivers appeared, grabbed hold of an arm apiece and forcibly dragged him away. As he made furious attempts to shake them off, a sheet of orange abruptly whooshed and enveloped the car. Ashley recoiled in horror. But the next instant stewards with extinguishers appeared and the fire was doused. Stunned, she gazed at the monitor. Everything seemed to have happened in excruciatingly slow motion, yet common sense said the entire incident could only have lasted seconds.

'The medical wagon's arrived,' the woman beside her said, but Ashley had grabbed up her jacket, jumped to her feet and was pushing her way out along the row.

When she reached the exit, she ran. Because she had been reluctant to meet up with Celeste again, she had sat in a public stand a long way away from the private seating, the grid, the pits, but now she raced back towards them. The ambulance would leave through that area, Ashley reasoned, so she would waylay it there and travel to the hospital with Simon. He would be seriously injured. He would need her. Passing hot-dog stands and car parks and stalls selling Formula One memorabilia, she sprinted around the outside of the circuit until, when her lungs felt as if they would burst, she finally reached double gates in the high chain-link perimeter fence which enclosed the pits.

'I have to go in,' Ashley gasped, as a security guard wandered forward to open them.

'Sorry, sweetheart, you need a pass,' he said, then gawked in surprise as she pushed past him and dashed straight through.

Deaf to his shouts, Ashley ran on to the service road. Where should she go? she wondered, her gaze travelling over tyre stores and fuel tanks, workshops and garages, parked cars and a village of motor-homes. An ambulance moved in the distance. Ashley swerved towards it, but as she ran the ambulance came to a halt beside a pad where a helicopter waited, a stretcher was ferried aboard and the helicopter rose up into the sky.

She stopped. 'No!' she wailed.

She would find a cab and follow Simon, Ashley decided, catching her breath, but she needed to know where he had been taken. Beside the helicopter pad a group of people were gathered and she jogged towards them. Drawing nearer, she saw that the group included mechanics, race officials and a number of drivers. Among them was Vitor, standing with the Dalgety executive whom she had met before. Her eyes widened in alarm. When he had attempted to release Simon he must have been hurt, for blood was forming crimson rivulets down one side of his face. She looked around for Celeste, but in vain. Where was she? Ashley wondered. Surely this was the time for his girlfriend to give Vitor all her support?

As she approached, the executive looked up.

'Vitor did his best, but tragically it was already too late,' he said, hurrying forward to place a protective arm around her.

'Too late?' An icy chill started at Ashley's heels and went all the way up her spine to the top of her head. 'Simon's. . .dead?' she asked haltingly.

'I'm afraid so. The only consolation is that he wouldn't have felt a thing. I'll get my car and run you back to your hotel. You'll want to call his folks and there are various matters to arrange — statements to the Press and so forth — but please be assured that Dalgety will provide all possible support.'

Ashley struggled to take in a situation which seemed totally unreal. 'Thank you,' she said.

The man turned to Vitor. 'Another chopper should be along for you at any minute, old chap, but why not go and wait in your van until it arrives?'

He nodded, then reached out to take hold of Ashley's arm.

'Come with me,' Vitor said.

Whatever had happened in the past, this was not the time to be aloof, Ashley thought, as she allowed him to lead her away. This was the time to offer mutual comfort.

'Would you like me to bathe your face?' she asked, when they reached the motorhome.

As though only now aware of his injuries, Vitor

touched his cheek. 'It's nothing,' he said, frowning at the blood he saw on his fingers. He gestured for her to sit on a cream leather banquette. 'You do realise what happened out there?' he demanded.

Ashley looked up at him. His eyes burned with a flinty light and his stance was rigid. Anger emanated from every pore. It was a legitimate reaction in the circumstances, she thought. Though, personally, she felt as if someone had injected her brain with a paralysing solution.

'Not exactly. I wasn't keeping too close a watch,' she confessed.

'Simon attempted to pass me on a bend, but he lost the back end of his car and all control. The gap was far too narrow and he was travelling much too fast, and there can only be one reason for him making such a damnfool, cavalier manoeuvre — he wasn't concentrating. You remember me telling you how crucial concentration is to a driver?' Vitor demanded. She nodded. 'So how come you follow him to Adelaide and, on the day before he's racing, you announce that you're pregnant?'

Ashley's mind seemed to implode. Simon had broken yesterday's confidences? He had informed Vitor that there was a possibility she might be having his child? Why had she been so foolishly frank? she wondered, cursing herself. She knew her foster brother was unreliable. But no wonder Vitor was furious. He would not have reckoned on their single liaison having such an outcome, and he would be blaming her for failing to have taken precautions. All right, there had been two of them involved and it was unfair, but he would be feeling tricked. . .and trapped.

'He — he told you?' she stammered, her voice faint with dismay.

'He did,' Vitor rasped.

Ashley cleared her throat. 'Nothing's certain yet.' She shone a shaky smile. 'It could be a false alarm.'

His reply was a derisory grunt. 'It must have occurred to you before you dropped your bombshell that it would distract Simon,' Vitor said, starting to pace up and down the confined space like an enraged tiger trapped in a too small cage. 'You must have realised that when you summoned him to your hotel to break the news——'

'You've got it wrong. For a start, I didn't summon him.' Neither did I follow him to Adelaide, Ashley thought belatedly. A mental note was made to correct the error as soon as she could. 'I spoke to him on the phone to complain about him putting my name in an article. He even gave the reporter a photograph of——'

'You sitting on his knee with your arm tight around his neck and laughing? I've seen it,' he cut in brusquely.

'Oh.' She frowned. The interruption had knocked her thoughts out of sync. 'I didn't summon Simon,' Ashley said, starting again. 'I rang him — he'd given me a list of all the Grands Prix contact numbers — but when he came to my hotel the next morning it was of his own accord.'

Vitor stopped his pacing to glare. 'And you were surprised?'

'Yes. I didn't expect him to come.'

In addition to explaining she was in Australia on business, Ashley had meant to say she had not broken the news, that Simon had guessed—but the moment seemed to have gone.

'It'd be a very odd individual who, when telephoned by his girlfriend and advised he was to be a father, failed to follow up on it,' Vitor growled, starting to walk again. 'This was the last race of the season, so all you had to do was wait one short day, bide your time for twenty-four hours, and the kid would have been home and dry.'

Her eyes opened wide. Vitor did not think she might be pregnant by him, Ashley realised numbly. He believed she was pregnant by Simon!

'You're mistaken,' she protested. 'I didn't tell Simon he could be going to be a father. I——'

She broke off in confusion. Her foster brother's misinformation must be dispelled, but what did she say? This did not seem a propitious moment for launching into an explanation of the possible repercussions of their lovemaking—and especially when she was having difficulty thinking.

'Don't try to wriggle your way out of it,' Vitor said stingingly.

Ashley's eyes were drawn to his torn face and the blood. The crimson rivulets were lengthening, tracing lines down his throat and soaking into the collar of his overalls. Surely his injuries must hurt? Didn't he feel the pain, the stickiness?

'I'm not,' she said.

'The fact that Simon worshipped the ground you

walked on means you must have been one hundred per cent certain that when you told him he'd insist on marrying you — which he did — so what difference did that one day make to you?' Vitor chopped down a hand in a savage gesture. 'None!'

'Simon said he was going to marry me?' she queried.

As she had fantasised about Vitor rethinking, so her foster brother seemed to have concocted a dream world of his own, Ashley thought bemusedly.

'He did. Telling him you were pregnant at that point in time was the height of selfishness,' he went on. 'It was callous and uncaring and despicable. If Simon hadn't had other things on his mind — if he hadn't been distracted by *you* — ' the word burst from him with a violence which made her recoil ' — he would never have made that fatal error.'

A knock sounded on the door. 'Ready to go, both of you,' the Dalgety man shouted.

'We're coming,' Vitor called back.

Ashley gazed at him, her thoughts in turmoil. 'You're accusing me of killing Simon,' she said, as the reason for his fury finally penetrated. 'You're wrong. I didn't distract him, I — '

'Don't fret,' he interjected harshly. 'I shan't be talking to the Press about it, nor to anyone else. What's the point? The kid's dead and it won't change anything.' Vitor's lips curled back from his teeth in contempt. 'However, don't you ever forget that I know who was responsible.'

Ashley did not forget — about Vitor d'Arcos's unjust accusation, nor about the man himself. How could she?

IT'S FUN! BIG BUCK$ IT'S FREE!

HOW TO PLAY

It's so easy...grab a lucky coin, and go right to your BIG BUCKS game card. Scratch off silver squares in a STRAIGHT LINE (across, down, or diagonal) until 5 dollar signs are revealed. BINGO!..Doing this makes you eligible for a chance to win $1,000,000.00 in lifetime income ($33,333.33 each year for 30 years)! Also scratch all 4 corners to reveal the dollar signs. This entitles you to a chance to win the $50,000.00 Extra Bonus Prize! Void if more than 9 squares scratched off.

Your EXCLUSIVE PRIZE NUMBER is in the upper right corner of your game card. Return your game card and we'll activate your unique Sweepstakes Number, so it's important that your name and address section is completed correctly. This will permit us to identify you and match you with any cash prize rightfully yours! (SEE BACK OF BOOK FOR DETAILS).—

FREE BOOKS PLUS FREE GIFTS!

At the same time you play your BIG BUCKS game card for BIG CASH PRIZES...scratch the Lucky Charm to receive FOUR FREE

Harlequin Presents® novels, and a FREE GIFT, TOO! They're totally free, absolutely free with no obligation to buy anything!

These books have a cover price of $3.50 each. But THEY ARE TOTALLY FREE; even the shipping will be at our expense! The Harlequin Reader Service® is not like some book clubs. You don't have to make any minimum number of purchases–not even one!

The fact is, thousands of readers look forward to receiving six of the best new romance novels each month and they love our discount prices!

Of course you may play BIG BUCKS for cash prizes alone by not scratching off your Lucky Charm, but why not get everything that we are offering and that you are entitled to! You'll be glad you did.

SER. 1.226

EXCLUSIVE PRIZE# 6M 625546

BIG BUCKS

Hurry!
This jackpot must be claimed!

Scratch Here →

LUCKY CHARM GAME!

WOW!
THEY'RE YOU!
1 FREE BOOK
AND A FREE GIFT!

Claim
• 4 FREE books
• AND a FREE Mystery Gift!

YES! I have played my BIG BUCKS game card as instructed. Enter my Big Bucks Prize number in the MILLION DOLLAR Sweepstakes III and also enter me for the Extra Bonus Prize. When winners are selected, tell me if I've won. If the Lucky Charm is scratched off, I will also receive everything revealed, as explained on the back and on the opposite page.

306 CIH AGTR
(C-H-P-08/94)

NAME _____

ADDRESS _____ APT. _____

CITY _____ PROV. _____ POSTAL CODE _____

NO PURCHASE OR OBLIGATION NECESSARY TO ENTER SWEEPSTAKES.

© 1993 HARLEQUIN ENTERPRISES LTD.

PRINTED IN U.S.A.

TWO WAYS TO WIN BIG BUCKS!

1. Uncover 5 $ signs in a row ... BINGO! You're eligible to win the $1,000,000.00 SWEEPSTAKES!

2. Uncover 5 $ signs in a row AND uncover $ signs in all 4 corners ... BINGO! You're also eligible for the $50,000.00 EXTRA BONUS PRIZE!

THE HARLEQUIN READER SERVICE®: HERE'S HOW IT WORKS

Accepting free books places you under no obligation to buy anything. You may keep the books and gift and return the shipping statement marked "cancel". If you do not cancel, about a month later we will send you 6 additional novels and bill you just $2.74 each plus 25¢ delivery and GST*. That's the complete price, and – compared to cover prices of $3.50 each – quite a bargain! You may cancel at any time, but if you choose to continue, every month we'll send you 6 more books, which you may either purchase at the discount price...or return at our expense and cancel your subscription.

*Terms and prices subject to change without notice. Canadian residents add applicable provincial taxes and GST.

0195619199-L2A5X3-BR01

"BIG BUCKS"
MILLION DOLLAR SWEEPSTAKES III
P.O. BOX 609
FORT ERIE, ONTARIO
L2A 9Z9

MAIL ⮞ POSTE
Canada Post Corporation / Société canadienne des postes
Postage paid   Port payé
if mailed in Canada   si posté au Canada
Business   Réponse
Reply   d'affaires
0195619199   01

CHAPTER FIVE

THE morning after Vitor's visit to her home, Ashley rang the local authority to enquire about her work licence. She was asked to hold and, after much background mumbling, the clerk advised her that the form she had submitted had regrettably been overlooked. However, it was now found and the licence would soon be with her. This was a relief, but a few days later, when Vitor's confirmation letter had been answered with a polite refusal, she started to worry again. Having been thwarted in his aims, was he going to swoop down at some unsuspected moment and engage her in another haranguing match? If so, her attitude would be light and bright, yet determined, Ashley resolved. Or might he think more about Thomas's colouring and return for a second, closer look? But after a month when Vitor failed to reappear she began to relax. He had, she decided, recognised that her business did not represent the handicap he had first imagined and abandoned his quest. Nor had any alarm bells rung about Thomas. Praise be.

But, although the construction company's overlord continued to stay away, a day or two later a gang of his labourers moved on to the land which surrounded her house. Energetic — and friendly whenever they came across her and Thomas — they set to work clearing it. Amid the undergrowth and beneath hedges, a collection of empty paint cans, old pieces of wood, discarded furniture and such was discovered. Ashley had not known the debris existed and watched in amazement as one refuse skip after another was filled.

Late one afternoon, when she returned with Thomas from the beach, a piece of paper had been pushed through her letterbox. As Ashley picked it up, her anxieties leapt into sudden life. Had Vitor called and might this be a note to warn he was due back? Should she turn right around and head for the safety of the beach again? But the paper proved to be a delivery docket. She was about to start painting a waterfall scene which would adorn the poolside of a new apartment complex in Praia do Carvoeiro and the special wave-embossed tiles which were to form the base of the picture had arrived. Ashley took a hasty look around, but failed to spot them. Never mind. The tiles would be located after dinner when Thomas, who was heavy-lidded and more than a little cranky, had been put to bed.

Later, as the day's heat faded into balminess and sunset streaked the sky with glorious shades of pink and gold, Ashley searched all around the house and up and down the drive, but the delivery seemed to have vanished. She gave a low growl of frustration. The tiles had taken a month to arrive, and if a replacement batch was required it would mean her hanging fire on the commission for another four weeks. Curses.

On the other side of the road at the front of the

house a builders' skip was full to the brim. Ashley walked across. She had looked everywhere else and, although it seemed a long shot, she might as well look in there. Hanging over the edge, she peered down. Buried beneath a fretwork of ancient planks, polythene sacks, and what looked like the treadle off a sewing machine, she saw a scruffy hessian-wrapped parcel. Eureka! Ashley wrinkled her nose. She might have found the dozen tiles, but now she had to retrieve them.

One plank was heaved off and she took a grip on another. 'Ouch!' she complained, as a nail jabbed into the soft pad of her thumb. More cautiously, she tried again, but the lower pieces of wood, which were as thick as roof beams, were wedged. Ashley set about unwedging them. She pushed and shoved. She grew hot and pink-faced and sweaty. But the timber remained jammed and the tiles continued to languish, tantalisingly so near and yet so far away. Wiping a slick of moisture from her brow, she reviewed the situation. If a grip could be got on the parcel, maybe she could thread it up between the wood and through?

Ashley was balanced on the edge of the skip with her arms stretching unsuccessfully down and her bottom stuck up in the air when, from the dark, smelly depths, she heard a car door slam. Abruptly conscious of the shortness of her shorts and the inelegance of her position, she pushed herself up and jumped down. As she turned, her heart kicked. The car was a black BMW and its driver was walking towards her. As before, Vitor D'Arcos looked impeccable in a pale blue shirt and dark pin-striped suit, though the jacket had been removed and was slung casually over one broad shoulder.

'*Boa noite*,' he said, grinning.

No doubt Vitor's amusement was inspired by the revealing view she had unwittingly provided for him, Ashley thought, rattled.

'*Boa noite*.' She wiped her hands on the backside of her shorts. 'And to what do I owe this pleasure?' she enquired, telling herself that she must be light and bright.

'Tomorrow I'm to take a look at some building plots which Paulo considers might be a good buy,' Vitor explained, 'So I arrived in Carvoeiro an hour ago and checked into my hotel. Then, as it's such a lovely evening——' he looked up at the painted sky '—I thought I'd wander along and see you.'

'To say that you've changed your mind about my workshop causing a disruption?' Ashley asked hopefully.

'No. I believe it will and it's still my intention to persuade you to sell.'

'That's persuade as in "batter me into submission"?' she questioned, with a smile.

'That's persuade as in "do whatever it takes",' Vitor replied, and jerked his head towards the skip. 'You were scavenging?' he enquired, as though he had not been in the least surprised to find her rummaging waist-deep through a multifarious pile of flotsam and jetsam.

Her smile narrowed. 'I was attempting to retrieve my own property,' Ashley said, and when he strode forward to look into the skip she pointed. 'You see the oblong package? It contains a delivery of tiles. For almost half an hour I've been trying to get them out, but it's impossible.'

'Hold this,' Vitor instructed, handing her his jacket. He took a grip on the timber and, tensing two muscled arms, lifted the whole load clear of the skip. He reached in. 'Here you are,' he said, passing her the tiles while he took back his jacket.

Ashley looked at him with wide, awed eyes. 'However did you manage that?' she enquired.

'I work out with weights — or I used to. I haven't been to a gym in ages,' Vitor said, and frowned as though the omission had only just occurred to him. 'What were the tiles doing in there?'

'I've no idea.' She shot him a suddenly suspicious look. 'This isn't the start of a campaign?' she asked.

'Campaign?'

'You could have told your men to try and make life difficult for me, in the hope that eventually I'll get so fed up that I'll accept your offer. What comes next?' Ashley demanded, her hazel eyes sparking as the idea gathered credibility. 'They create the maximum amount of noise, dust, disturbance? They dig trenches which make it difficult for me to get out? They accidentally, on purpose, cut off my water or the electricity?'

Not in the least moved by her show of temper, Vitor wagged a finger. 'What a wicked mind,' he chided. 'Do you honestly believe I'd be stupid enough to involve my employees in actions which would create talk and could damage the reputation of my company?'

She scuffed the toe of a flip-flop in the dust. 'No,' Ashley admitted.

'Where were the tiles to begin with?' he enquired.

'I don't know. All I know is that they were delivered.'

'So the driver could have left them outside your front wall?'

'I guess,' she conceded.

'The wrapping's second-hand,' Vitor continued, looking at the hessian, 'and if some guy was being super-efficient he could have decided that whatever it was which had been dumped on the road it should be tidied away.'

'It's possible.'

'It's probable,' he countered.

Ashley felt compromised by her previous suspicions. They had been a knee-jerk reaction, the result of her feeling unsettled by Vitor's reappearance.

'I shouldn't have been so. . .hostile,' she mumbled.

'No, you shouldn't. After all, you're the one who suggested we be friends.' Reaching out, Vitor touched a honey-coloured strand of hair which had tumbled from her topknot to curl down over the exposed nape of her neck. 'Which suits me fine,' he murmured, twisting the tendril around his finger.

The casual intimacy of his gesture was seductive, likewise the husky timbre of his voice. Instead of battering, might he have decided to try and sweet-talk her into submission? Ashley wondered. Alarm twanged at her nerves. Vitor d'Arcos was a man who could woo. Even more dangerous, he was a man who *knew* he could woo. But she needed his goodwill.

'Would you like a drink?' Ashley enquired, remembering to be light and bright, and thinking how Thomas was safely tucked up in bed..

His brows arched in mock-disdain. 'You're being very gracious with me this evening.'

'I thought the weary traveller might be dehydrated again,' she said.

'He is, and thanks. If you want to make a start painting, I'm happy to take my drink into your workshop,' Vitor said, as they walked up the drive.

Ashley shook her head. 'The evening's half gone and I'm on schedule, so I shan't bother working tonight.'

'Lucky you. There's a pile of papers which I must read when I get back to the hotel,' he said, and grimaced. 'I was hoping to look at them on the plane, but they were at the bottom of the pile and I never got around to it.'

'Which plane?' she enquired.

'The one from Brazil. I landed in Lisbon at lunchtime.'

'And then you drove straight down here?' Ashley protested, leading him into the house and through to the living-room.

Vitor jettisoned his jacket. 'Not straight down.' Dropping his long frame into an overstuffed arm-chair, he stretched up his arms and yawned. 'I called into the office first to bring myself up to date.'

She had not noticed before, but now Ashley saw that his face was gaunt and there were dark circles beneath his eyes. He looked tired and overburdened.

'Did you sleep on the plane?' she asked.

'I had a couple of hours, but the paperwork needed my attention, so——' His shoulders rose and wearily fell.

'What can I get you?' she enquired. 'There's lager, as before, or chilled white wine, or——'

'Wine would be great, thanks.'

'Do you do the journey to Brazil often?' Ashley called, as she opened the bottle in the kitchen.

There was no reply, and when she returned to the living-room she found Vitor sprawled in the arm-chair, fast asleep.

Putting his glass down on the low coffee-table, Ashley sat quietly in a corner of the sofa. Strands of dark hair had fallen over his brow and his lashes were feathered on his cheeks. Vitor looked younger and surprisingly vulnerable when he was asleep, she thought. A hand squeezed at her heart. He also looked very much like Thomas.

Ashley took a shaky breath. Common decency insisted that Vitor must be told he had a son. He possessed a basic human right and she had already held back too long. Far too long. But if she revealed the truth, what then? Would he publicly acknowledge the little boy as his, or might he prefer to ignore his existence? Playing with Thomas for five minutes was one thing; being saddled with a lifetime interest in an offspring was another.

She swallowed down a mouthful of wine. If Vitor chose to take an interest, what would it entail? she brooded, as she had brooded over the subject a thousand times before. Would he be content to leave her in charge of Thomas and merely check on his progress from time to time, or might he endeavour to wield control in her—his—*their* son's life? On learning that the child carried his genes, might he take her to court and attempt to gain custody? Ashley's fingers tightened involuntarily around the glass. Would he win? His lawyer could argue that, while she was a loving and competent mother, other circumstances should be considered. Like Vitor's wealth. The millions he had earned from Formula One added to the money he must be making now meant he could provide Thomas with cast-iron financial security, an exceedingly comfortable home and a first-class education. Plus a connoisseur's collection of toy cars, Ashley thought grimly. Whereas, although not impoverished, she would always have to watch the pennies.

If Vitor did take her to court it would be in Portugal, where she was a foreigner and where he must have all kinds of contacts, muscle, sway. Ashley frowned. Should she sell him the house and take the first flight back to England? she wondered. Would she and Thomas be safer there? She stared down into her glass. There were so many questions—all unanswerable. So many ifs. So many buts. A sense of fatality gripped her. The obligation to alert Vitor to his paternity had stalked her since the day of Thomas's birth, but now it was breathing down her neck. Breathing hotly. Her inherent sense of duty insisted that, whatever the risks, whatever the dangers, she *must* speak.

'Is something wrong?'

At the question, her head jerked up and she saw that Vitor had awakened from his nap and was frowning at her.

'Nothing,' Ashley said quickly. She paused, then gave a wavering smile. 'Actually I was thinking about Thomas.'

He came to sit beside her.

'Is he ill?' Vitor asked, his tone was concerned.

'No, no, he's perfectly healthy,' she assured him.

What did she say next? Ashley wondered, struck by a sudden heart-banging, blood-curdling terror. Did she wade straight in with a blunt announcement or should she try to approach the subject from a more oblique angle which might encourage him to guess? After all, it must have crossed his mind — just once — that the timing of their lovemaking made it possible for Thomas to have been his?

'Looking after a child on your own can't be easy,' Vitor said. 'You must worry like hell at times.'

'I do,' she agreed.

'And you're worrying now?'

If only you knew how much! she thought. 'Yes,' Ashley said wanly.

'Try not to. Thomas is a bright kid and tough. I've no doubt he'll have all the usual childhood ailments and get into more than a few scrapes, but he'll survive,' Vitor said, with a smile of encouragement.

'I know. It's not that I'm worrying about. It's——'

She stopped dead, unable to prise out the words which could jeopardise the life that she and Thomas shared, which could wreck the child's emotional stability she had worked so hard to ensure, which could take him away.

Vitor put his arm around her. 'Imagining things is much worse than the reality,' he told her.

'Always?' Ashley asked.

'Always.' Lifting a hand, he ran his knuckles down the smoothness of her cheek. 'So cheer up.'

She wished he were not being so kind, so tender— even if it was because he hoped to cajole her into selling him her house. She also wished she could put off telling him until tomorrow. Or next week. Or next year. But she could not put it off forever.

'I'm trying,' Ashley said.

Vitor grinned crookedly. 'Try harder,' he appealed and, taking her wine glass from her and putting it on the table, he drew her close.

Ashley rested her head against his shoulder. She knew it was illogical, but she craved to be held, to be comforted—by him. She craved his strength and his solidity. Just for a moment.

She took a breath. 'About my imaginings,' she began, 'I——'

'Shh.' He kissed her brow. 'Forget them.'

'But——'

Vitor kissed the tip of her nose. 'I said forget. I mean it.'

Ashley tried again. 'Vitor, you don't——'

'Ashley, I do,' he said, gently mocking. 'Stop frowning,' he ordered, kissing her brow a second time, 'and smile.'

As if intent on persuading her lips to curve, he bent and kissed first one corner of her mouth and then the other. When he drew back and his eyes lingered on her mouth, Ashley knew he was tempted to kiss her again — properly. Her heart began a slow, heavy pounding. Leif had talked of her having needs, and now she needed Vitor to kiss her. Very much. She also wanted him to undress her and make wild passionate love. Wrong, Ashley thought. She was not going to fall into the trap of thinking she wanted Vitor as Vitor. After two years without having felt a man's arms around her, she was vulnerable, and what she wanted was any suitably attractive and virile male.

Ashley sat forward and picked up her glass of wine. Those two years had also made her wiser and a darn sight more wary so, vulnerable or not, there was no way she would risk another close encounter of the erotic kind. That wildfire feeling might have got a hold a month back, but it would not be allowed to do so again. Vitor might be her weak spot, but *she* was not going to be weak.

'You enquired about men friends once,' Ashley said brightly. 'I'm friendly with Leif.'

Vitor frowned. 'Leif?' he questioned.

'He's a good-looking Danish guy who installs kitchens. I told you that I do business for him,' she said, and explained.

'You're dating the guy?'

'Not exactly, it's difficult to organise a babysitter. But we see each other three or four times a week.' Ashley took a sip of wine. 'How's Celeste?' she enquired, in a deliberate reminder of his girlfriend.

'The last I heard she was fine,' Vitor said, reaching for his glass.

'The two of you have split up?' she asked.

'Didn't Simon tell you?'

'Simon?' Her brow crinkled. 'You mean you split up before he was killed?'

Vitor nodded. 'I ended the relationship shortly after the Portuguese Grand Prix two years back.'

Ashley darted him a look from beneath her lashes. In other words, he had broken with the model after their blink-of-the-eye affair. Had it had any bearing?

'Celeste must have been very upset,' she remarked.

'Only for as long as it took her to latch on to another driver,' Vitor said drily.

'But she seemed so——'

'Celeste was never in love with me, it was the idea of me that she loved. And the travel and the glamour of Formula One.' He cast her a look. 'You weren't particularly impressed either with racing or with me as a driver, were you?'

Ashley shook her head. 'Why did you give up Formula One?' she enquired. She hesitated, aware of asking a question which had the power to explode in her face. 'Was it because of Simon's death?'

Stretching out his legs, Vitor frowned down at his feet. 'It jolted me into making the decision to quit, but I'd been moving that way for a long time. I'd never enjoyed the media interest and the goldfish-bowl aspect of driving, and while I was grateful to have fans their continual invasion of my privacy got me down. But the main reason for quitting was that I felt stale, burnt-out. The joy had gone. I hid it from everyone,' he said, when her brows rose in surprise, 'and for a long time I hid it from myself. With hindsight, it's clear that I was *too* single-minded about racing, *too* immersed, and that if I'd paced myself better the joy would have lasted much longer.' He took a swig from his glass and grinned. 'Anyhow, I find what I'm doing now far more stimulating and far more personally worthwhile. Like you, I enjoy running my own business.'

'As you were too single-minded about racing, aren't you in danger of becoming too single-minded about your construction company?' Ashley suggested.

He shook his head. 'No chance.'

'Think about it. You said you hadn't been to a gym in ages. When did you last go to the theatre, out to dinner, have a holiday?' she enquired.

Vitor pursed his lips. 'I haven't done any of them for a long time. For two years,' he admitted.

'I made that mistake once, but you should widen your interests, cut down on the travel and delegate more,' she told him, her expression serious. 'Apart from burn-out, working such long hours can't be good for you. Maybe all that happens now is that you feel tired, but give it a year or two and——'

'You'd better watch yourself,' Vitor said drily,

'you're softening.' Draining his glass, he rose to his feet. 'Thanks for the drink, but my paperwork awaits.'

The reference to Simon's death had not brought accusations raining down on her head, Ashley reflected when her visitor had driven away. Granted, Vitor continued to blame her, but it represented some kind of progress. She must explain about Simon, she resolved. Her hazel eyes clouded. And she must, she *must*, tell him the truth about Thomas.

Having decided that it would take at least a month for Praia do Carvoeiro to be slotted into Vitor's hectic schedule again, Ashley was surprised when the black BMW drew up outside her house a couple of weeks later. She was standing on the drive, reaching the end of a discussion about a kitchen order with Leif, and as Vitor climbed from the car she felt herself grow tense. His appearance was a stark reminder that although a fortnight ago he had distracted her from telling him about Thomas — or maybe she had chickened out? — the revelation *had* to be faced.

But, although Ashley stood still and wary, her son showed no inhibitions. He had been playing on the terrace, but he clambered to his feet and, yelling, 'Mo' car,' hurtled down the drive as fast as his little legs would carry him. Vitor grinned and held his arms out wide, and Thomas ran straight into them.

'Hello, trouble,' Vitor said, lifting him up. He tickled his tummy. 'How's about you and me having a sit in my car?'

The little boy squirmed with delight. 'Pease,' he said.

A lump formed in Ashley's throat. She needed to blink away tears. Whatever the difficulties which lay in wait, she could not help but be touched by this meeting of her son with his father.

'Is that guy a relative?' Leif demanded, as Vitor sat in the driving seat with the child on his knee.

She looked at him in alarm. While Thomas had inherited her nose and her chin, the likeness to Vitor was apparent in the shape and darkness of his eyes, in the line of his mouth. To her their kinship was obvious, but she had thought it was because she *knew*—yet Leif also appeared to have detected it.

'A relative?' Ashley asked, her heart racing in near-panic.

'Thomas seems to know him well, so I thought maybe he was a cousin of yours or something.'

She gave a burst of shrill laughter. 'No, that's Vitor D'Arcos. You remember, I told you it's his company which is building the villas?'

'And how he was Simon's team-mate? Yes. I should have recognised him, but it's a while since I've seen his picture.' Leif frowned at the toddler who was happily clutching at the steering-wheel. 'Thomas is far friendlier towards him than he is towards me.'

Which is because *you* are not friendly towards Thomas, Ashley thought. Vitor's tactile greeting had made a sharp contrast with the gruff 'hello' which Leif had bestowed earlier, before turning all his attention to her. She had believed Thomas was shy of the Dane, but now she realised that the child gave nothing out because he received nothing back in return.

'It's the car Thomas likes,' she said placatingly.

'How often has D'Arcos been here?' Leif demanded, as if sensing a challenger for her affections.

'Just a couple of times. As I explained, he wants to buy my house. Thanks,' Ashley said, as Vitor came up the drive with Thomas prancing in front of him, 'you've made one little boy very happy.'

He grinned. 'Anything to please.'

'This is Leif. Leif Haraldsen,' she explained, and introduced the two men.

'Had any further trouble with things going missing in skips?' Vitor asked, when he and the Dane had shaken hands.

Ashley gave a shamefaced smile. 'None.'

'Are you intending to make Ashley another offer for her house?' Leif demanded.

Vitor frowned, as though he objected both to the direct approach and to the Dane's knowledge of her affairs.

'As a matter of fact, that's why I'm here.'

'And the offer is?' Ashley enquired.

The look Vitor shot her said he would prefer to discuss the matter in private. In truth, that was her preference, too. She was not particularly eager to share the information with Leif — though doubtless he would bombard her with searching questions, as he had done before — but she had made Vitor think that the two of them were close.

Vitor named an even larger sum.

She smiled. 'Thanks, but no, thanks.'

'You're turning down a sum like that?' Leif protested, swinging to her in disbelief. 'But if you got that for this place and I sold my apartment, together we'd have enough money to get married and buy——' He broke off, a flush appearing beneath his tan as he realised he was pushing her too far along the relationship path and could also be sounding mercenary. He inspected his watch. 'I have an appointment in fifteen minutes in Lagoa, so I must go.'

With a smile at Ashley, a curt nod for Vitor, and ignoring Thomas entirely, he strode off to his van.

'I thought you reckoned he was good-looking,' Vitor remarked, as the Dane drove away.

'He is.'

'Huh, with those blue eyes, the tan and the toothpaste smile, he reminds me of a game-show host.' He nodded towards Thomas, who had wandered off to squat down on the terrace and poke at something at the foot of the vines. 'He doesn't think much of the guy either.'

'Maybe not,' Ashley said stiffly. 'However, I happen to like him. What is that?' she enquired, when Thomas gave a sudden chortle.

She walked forward to investigate, but as she did the object of the little boy's interest crept out into full view. As Ashley stared in horror at the hairy black spider, Thomas extended a curious finger.

'Don't!' Vitor commanded.

In quick strides, he came forward, scooped the child from the ground and thrust him at her. He looked around, grabbed up a discarded gardening trowel and, as the spider crawled across the stone flagging, he whacked it.

'It was a tarantula!' Ashley exclaimed, frowning down at the corpse. She hugged Thomas close to her. 'He could have been killed!'

Vitor shook his head. 'It was too small to have done him much harm.'

'But it could have been a big spider,' she said, her tone distraught as she imagined what might have happened.

'But it wasn't,' he said soothingly. 'And if you explain to Thomas that he's not to touch things like that, but must come and tell you when he finds one, then he'll avoid any danger in future.'

'I suppose so,' she admitted.

A dark brow lifted. 'Well?' he said.

'Well what?' Ashley asked.

'Aren't you going to heap the blame on me? Aren't you going to claim that the spider must have been disturbed when the undergrowth was cleared and so it was all my fault?' Vitor demanded, a bite in his voice.

Ashley looked at him. She was not going to jump to any more dubious conclusions. She refused to make any further wild and unfair assertions. At one time she might have considered Vitor to be a dyed-in-the-wool monster, but she was gradually reassessing her opinion.

'If I do, will you say that if I don't want to risk any similar events the solution is for me to move?' she responded.

He shook his head. 'I wouldn't say that.'

'Nor am I blaming you. It's well over a week since the last patch of ground was cleared and a spider turning up is pure chance.' Ashley hesitated. 'Though I'd be grateful if you could have a look around the vines to make sure there aren't any more.'

'Will do,' Vitor agreed, and checked under and through the foliage. 'All clear,' he reported.

'Thanks. You're wearing jeans,' she said, all of a sudden.

'Full marks for observation,' Vitor said drily. 'I'm also wearing a sports shirt and trainers, like you. And the reason is that, as well as coming to have my offer for your house refused, yet again,' he said pithily, 'I'm also here to invite you and Thomas to lunch on the quay in Portimão.'

Her and Thomas, that made a change, Ashley thought. On the occasions when Leif had attempted to fix a date — sometimes a lunch date — the little boy had never been included.

'But what about your work?' she protested.

'You said I was too single-minded about it and should widen my interests, so I am. How do you fancy going for a ride in my car?' he asked Thomas. 'I've bought you a safety seat and fitted it in the back.' He looked at her. 'How about lunch?'

'As you've gone to so much trouble, it would seem discourteous to refuse,' Ashley said.

Vitor grinned. 'It would seem damned annoying.'

With Thomas sitting gleeful and beaming like a

miniature king in the newly acquired seat, they set off.

'Paulo told me that the Festa de Barcos, the blessing of the boats, is being held in Carvoeiro this morning,' Vitor remarked, the car gathering speed. 'Have you seen the ceremony?'

Ashely shook her head. 'No. I've heard about it, but I wasn't aware that it was happening today.'

Like every country, Portugal had its own traditions, its own festivals, its own special holidays — such as when independence from the Spanish back in 1640 was celebrated, or the more recent revolution was remembered — but she had yet to fix the dates in her mind.

'Shall we take a detour and go and look?' he suggested. 'It should be starting around now.'

She grinned. 'Yes, please.'

On the headland above Praia do Carvoeiro and overlooking the sea sat the small white local church. Crowds of spectators were thronging the sides of the narrow road which led down from it into the village and, after Vitor had hurriedly found a parking place, they joined them. They were only just in time, for a minute or two later a procession appeared at the top of the hill and began to make its way slowly down.

Vitor lifted Thomas into his arms.

'See the priests?' he said, indicating the clergymen in their flowing richly coloured robes who came first. He nodded towards a statue of the Virgin Mary which was being carried on high. 'And the Madonna?'

'Donna,' the little boy repeated, his brown eyes large with interest.

Next the choir in ankle-length cassocks walked solemnly past, followed by the children of the congregation, all with faces scrubbed, hair well brushed and dressed in their best. Proud parents and a mass of other churchgoers came in their wake. The Portuguese were very fond of children, Ashley reflected, glancing at Vitor, who was telling Thomas all about the ceremony.

'Now the chief priest is going to say a prayer for the boats on the beach,' he explained, as they went with other spectators to join in behind the end of the procession and follow it across the square and on to the sand.

The village boasted a fleet of a dozen or so small fishing boats, which Ashley had seen setting sail at night and returning with their slippery silver haul in the mornings. Each boat had been freshly painted in bright colours for the occasion, and beside them stood their sinewy weather-beaten owners. As the choristers sang a low chant in the background, the priest moved from one vessel to the next, praying for the fishermen to be kept safe from harm, and asking that the catch over the next year may be bountiful. To Ashley the ceremony seemed a simple and yet moving reminder of the basics of life.

'Thank you, I enjoyed being a part of that,' she said gravely, as the procession wended its way off around the village before finally returning to the church.

'And now you've built up an appetite for sampling some of the fish which may have been brought ashore here?' Vitor asked.

She grinned. 'A hearty one.'

CHAPTER SIX

WHEN they arrived in Portimão, a bustling fishing port some ten miles to the west of Praia do Carvoeiro, the tables which sat in rows in front of the quayside restaurants had already begun to fill. While dishes such as sole, sea bream and lobster featured on the menu, the lunchtime speciality was sardines. Not the tiny ones which came packed tight in tins, but a fresh plump eight- or nine-inch variety which were grilled over charcoal in the open air. Served with new potatoes and a mixed salad, they made a tasty meal and proved a constant draw to holidaymakers and locals alike.

The small restaurants were in good-natured competition to secure the most customers, and as Ashley and Vitor approached waiters came out to greet them. With many smiles, they were enticed to sample the *sardinhas grelhadas* from *this* smoking barbecue, to choose *this* table, to patronise *this* establishment which, it was winsomely claimed, provided the choicest view of the sparkling blue mouth of the Arade river.

'You need a highchair,' declared a long-aproned and straw-boatered young man, grinning down at Thomas in his buggy. 'I have a highchair.' He bowed. 'If *senhor* and *senhora* would care to come this way——'

Seconds later, they were installed at an umbrella-shaded table with the little boy sitting in state alongside.

Because Vitor had thanked him in his own language, the waiter took them both to be fellow compatriots and proceeded to chatter away in Portuguese, remarking on the sunny weather, suggesting choices of food and wine, complimenting them on Thomas's cuteness and good behaviour.

'He thinks we're married and that Thomas is mine,' Vitor commented, when the young man had taken their orders and rushed off. He gave a wry smile. 'Which is only natural, I suppose.'

Ashley made an indistinct murmur. Why had she been so receptive to this lunch date? she wondered belatedly. Why had she exposed herself to the danger of someone remarking on the likeness between her son and her escort, and making the obvious connection? Picking up the menu, she took an avid interest in the desserts.

'Thomas likes *pudim flan* and if I'm not too full maybe I'll have. . . What's *pudim Molotov*?' she enquired.

'An egg-white mousse with toffee sauce.'

'Sounds delicious.'

'It is.' Vitor's brown eyes trapped hers. 'Thomas could be mine,' he said.

Ashley's stomach hollowed. Although she had half hoped he might guess, she did not want him to guess *now*, she thought frantically. Not when they were in a public place and surrounded by other people. Not when Thomas might pick up the emotional currents. All right, the little boy would not understand, but——

'Apart from the fact that you were three months pregnant at the time of Simon's death,' Vitor completed.

Her mind kicked and bucked. 'Simon told you that?' she said wonderingly.

He nodded. 'Looks promising,' he agreed, turning to speak to the waiter, who had arrived to brandish a bottle of the red wine which he had so enthusiastically recommended.

As the wine was uncorked and Vitor was invited to sample it, Ashley's gaze swung away. A chain of fishermen were unloading baskets of crabs from a boat moored against the quay; beyond this others sat mending their nets in the sunshine, and further along signs extolled holidaymakers to experience the splendours of deep-sea fishing. She saw nothing. If Vitor believed her to have been three months pregnant in Adelaide, then he believed she had already been pregnant when they had made love! Now she understood his failure to add two and two and make the obvious four; it was due to Simon doctoring the facts. Yet again, her supposed boyfriend had lied. Yet again, he had caused trouble. Her heart sank. Yet again, it was a falsehood which she would need to explain and correct.

Reaching for a napkin, Ashley tucked it beneath Thomas's chin. She refused to think about Simon's skulduggery—or any corrections—now. This was the first time she and her son had been wined and dined since coming to live in Portugal and she was determined to enjoy it.

Thanks to the delicious food, the relaxed out-of-doors location and Vitor's good humour, enjoyment was not a problem. Throughout the meal the conversation flowed pleasantly, amusingly and — to Ashley's continual relief — unthreateningly.

'The other day Thomas and I went over to look at the foundations of the first villa which your men have started to build,' she remarked, as they drank their coffee. 'It's going to be spacious.'

Vitor nodded. 'The house is the largest of the five different styles.' Taking a ballpoint pen from his shirt pocket, he began to sketch on the paper table-cover. 'This is what it'll look like from the front. We've tried to blend the traditional Moorish style with modern refinements,' he explained, drawing a clean-lined villa with a pillared front door, wrought-iron balcony rails and pretty lacework chimneys.

'Elegant,' Ashley said admiringly. 'And what's the floor plan?'

Vitor drew it out. 'In addition to the living-room, dining-room and the study, there's this extra room downstairs,' he said, showing her. 'It could be used as an additional bedroom, or a television den——'

'Or a playroom,' she suggested, wiping remains of caramel custard from around Thomas's mouth.

'Whatever. More coffee?' he enquired.

'No, thanks.'

Vitor's lips twitched. 'How about a second *pudim Molotov*?' he suggested.

Ashley groaned and put a hand to her stomach. 'It was gorgeous, but I couldn't.'

Attracting the waiter's attention, he scribbled in the air. '*A Conta, por favor,*' he requested.

'Thank you for a lovely meal,' she said, when Vitor had settled the bill and they were walking back along the quay. 'I used to go out on Sundays in London, sometimes to a brasserie in Covent Garden or to an "olde Englishe" pub, and I'd forgotten just how pleasant a long lunch can be.'

'But you never get homesick?'

'Yes, I do,' Ashley admitted. 'Last month someone brought a red double-decker London bus down to the Algarve to promote British goods, and when I saw it I almost cried.' She gave a rueful smile. 'Homesickness only strikes occasionally now, but when I first arrived in February and setting up home here seemed so alien I was often mopey.'

'The almond blossoms didn't help?' Vitor asked.

Ashley cast him a quizzical look. 'I don't know what you mean.'

'There's a legend which says that, once upon a time, a handsome and passionate Moorish king won the hand of a lovely princess from a northern country and brought her to live on the Algarve,' Vitor explained. 'However, although he lavished all his love and many gifts on his adored wife, she seemed to be unhappy. When he asked her why, she shyly confessed that she was pining for the snows of her native land. On hearing this, the king gave orders for the fields around his castle to be planted with almond trees for as far as the eye could see. The next February he awakened his bride from her melancholy sleep and carried her over to the window, where, on looking out, she saw the landscape covered in white. The sea of almond blossoms, the gift of her loving husband, cured her homesickness in a flash.'

Ashley sighed. The next time she admired the Algarve's famous springtime extravaganza, it would have warmly romantic connotations.

'And they lived happily ever after?' she enquired.

Vitor smiled. 'Naturally. How do you fancy a drive up to Caldas de Monchique?' he suggested, when they reached the car.

Her thoughts went to the sleepy mountain village with its wooded hillsides and ancient Roman spa. Caldas had once been a favourite family haunt, she recalled wistfully, and had the local bus service not meandered into every far-flung hamlet on its way and taken forever to make the journey she would have been back long ago. Forget house improvements; her next priority would be to buy a car, Ashley decided. In addition to its hundred or so miles of beaches, the Algarve boasted all manner of interesting places, and it was a crime that she and Thomas were unable to visit them.

'I fancy it very much,' she said, and checked her watch, 'but it's well past three and it's a long drive to Lisbon, so shouldn't you make a start?'

'I'm not going back today,' Vitor told her. 'I'm spending the night down here and returning in the morning.'

Ashley grinned. She had some tiles to paint, but

they could be done tomorrow. 'Then Caldas would be great.'

On the road again, she waited for Thomas to go to sleep. He had not had his usual nap, so surely the rhythm of the car would lull him? It did not. As Vitor drove up into the mountains, the little boy remained bright-eyed and wide-awake. He was, it seemed, determined not to miss a single minute of their day out. As they walked uphill from the spa, beneath the shade of chestnut trees and beside a crystal-clear stream, Thomas did not flag. Nor when, a couple of hours later, they travelled back south towards the coast and took a detour into Silves.

Once a medieval city of magnificent palaces, gardens and bazaars, Silves was now a provincial backwater; with only a Moorish fortress and twelfth-century cathedral to remind visitors of its former greatness. As the afternoon lapsed into evening, they explored the huge fort and later admired the faded opulence of the church.

'Why don't we bring our sightseeing to an end with an early dinner?' Vitor suggested, when they emerged on to the cobbled streets again. 'It'd save you having to make anything at home.'

Ashley grinned. It was fun being out and about. 'Yes, please,' she said.

Although Thomas had begun to rub small fists into his eyes, he managed to stay awake while they ate omelettes in a local tavern. But this time on their return to the car he fell fast asleep within minutes.

Leaden clouds had rolled in with the setting sun

and as they neared Carvoeiro fat drops of rain began to splash on to the windscreen.

'I've had a great time,' Ashley said, thanking Vitor when he brought the car to a halt. She looked back at the comatose Thomas and smiled. 'So has he.'

'Likewise,' Vitor told her. 'If you'd like to unfasten Rip van Winkle, I'll get the buggy from the boot,' he offered, and together they climbed out into the now steady downpour.

Hurriedly opening the rear door, Ashley bent inside. 'We're home,' she said, when Thomas's eyelids drowsily lifted. She released the straps and took a hold of him. 'Out you come.'

The toddler instantly stiffened and went as rigid as a board. 'No,' he protested.

''Fraid so,' Ashley said, feeling the rain on her jeans.

'No!' When she began to lift him, he flung out his arms and batted her away. 'No! No! No!'

'I realise you love this car and I know you're tired,' she said, determinedly hauling him out, 'but I'd be grateful if you could save this until we're in the house and in the dry.'

Thomas kicked his legs. He went red in the face. He yelled.

'He doesn't usually throw tantrums,' Ashley said ruefully, as Vitor came round from the boot, 'but he has had a very long day.' She struggled to hold the wriggling squealing child. 'You go. Don't get wet. If you give me the buggy, I'll be fine.'

He shook his head. 'I'll bring in the buggy and I'll

carry him,' he said, and before she could protest he had taken Thomas from her. 'Run,' Vitor instructed, and as Ashley obediently turned and headed off up the drive he sprinted beside her.

Indoors, she flicked the rain from her hair and switched on the lights. It was not properly dark, but the bad weather had made the evening gloomy.

'We're in for a storm,' Ashley remarked, grimacing as thunder rumbled in the distance. She eyed Thomas. 'I'll give you a quick bath and then it's straight to bed.'

The little boy had been momentarily subdued in Vitor's arms, but now he took a breath. 'No!' he bawled, going red in the face again. 'No!'

Vitor held out a hand. 'Give me five,' he said.

The bawling came to an abrupt end as Thomas frowned first at him and then down at his hand.

'How many fingers do you have?' Vitor enquired. 'One, two, three, four, *five*,' he said, counting them.

'Five,' the child echoed, still frowning.

A streak of lightning split the sky. Rain lashed noisily at the windows.

'So when I say "give me five", you slap your fingers on mine, like this,' Vitor told him, and demonstrated. 'Now—give me five.'

Thomas chuckled. 'Five!' he carolled, and slammed his little hand down on Vitor's big one. ''Gain,' he demanded instantly.

'Give me five,' Vitor said. 'Do you want to get his bath ready?' he suggested, as Thomas laughed and repeated the action.

Ashley smiled. 'Yes—and many thanks.'

As she made her way to the blue and white tiled bathroom which was at the other end of the house, there was another clap of thunder and the lightning flashed again. Turning on the brass taps, she half filled the bath with warm water. Ashley had collected Thomas's pyjamas from his bedroom and was about to fetch him when the lights suddenly went out.

'Not guilty,' Vitor called, from the living-room.

She laughed. 'It's a power-cut; they happen quite often during storms,' Ashley told him, shouting back down the darkened hallway. 'They don't usually last for long, but I'm prepared. There are candles strategically placed, so I'll fix things in here and then come through to you.'

On the windowsill, coloured candles sat ready and waiting in old pewter candlesticks. Ashley located the matches, which were kept out of harm's way in the medicine cabinet, lit the wicks and placed the candles at intervals around the room. Their flickering light showed her the way down the hall to where she placed another candle in an alcove and then, with matches in hand, she walked towards the living-room.

On the threshhold, Ashley paused. Through the shadows, she saw Vitor sitting in an armchair with Thomas. The child lay quietly against his chest, on the brink of sleep and so obviously relishing their closeness. She had relished the closeness which the three of them had shared today, she thought pensively. She had liked them being regarded as a

family. It had been comforting. Sustaining. Safe.
Her heart suddenly felt heavy. But it was a pretence.

Ashley stepped forward. 'If I light the big candle
on the mantelpiece and put a couple on the bureau
that's usually enough,' she said, flourishing the
matchbox.

'Shall I do them?' Vitor offered.

'Er—shouldn't you be going?' she suggested awk-
wardly—and hopefully.

She did not want any more pretend closeness, any
more sham togetherness. Neither did she want to be
alone with him in the dark.

'If it's all right by you, I'll wait a few minutes until
the storm subsides,' Vitor said, as thunder boomed
again.

Her stomach clenched. 'It's all right by me,'
Ashley replied brightly. 'Bathtime,' she announced,
and, marching forward, she lifted Thomas from his
knee.

In the bathroom, she undressed the little boy and
washed him. Usually he liked to play, but tonight he
was too tired, and so, wasting no time, Ashley lifted
him out again. She was kneeling beside the child,
putting on his pyjamas, when Vitor appeared in the
doorway. Her nerves jangled. She would have preferred it if he had remained in the living-room. She
would prefer him to keep away from her.

'It looks romantic,' Vitor remarked, his eyes travelling around.

The light from the half-dozen candles was flickering over the glossy surface of the *azulejos*—the
traditional blue and white tiles which, in Portugal,

covered the walls of palaces and cottages alike. It cast dancing shadows on the thick white carpet and gilded the green leaves of the plants which spilled from ceramic pots.

'Yes,' Ashley agreed, with a tight smile.

'I'd like to have a bath in here in the candlelight,' he said quietly. He paused. 'With you.'

She had been fastening the buttons at the shoulder of Thomas's elephant-patterned pyjamas, but all sense of co-ordination suddenly seemed to vanish and her fingers fumbled in vain. As Ashley looked up at him, she gulped in a breath. The air had gone heavy, still, felt super-charged.

'I'd like to undress you very slowly,' he continued, his dark eyes steady on hers, 'and press my lips to every inch of your skin which is revealed. Then I'd like you to undress me and kiss every inch of me. When we're both naked, I'd like to take you into the water and soap you. Soap your breasts until I feel your nipples hard against my palms.'

Ashley made a frantic attack on the buttons again. To her dismay, her body was reacting to the sensual word pictures Vitor had created and she could feel herself becoming aroused. As he spoke his eyes had fallen and she knew that from the centre of each perfectly round breast a peak jutted, lifting the thin material of her shirt. She had no need to look down; she could feel the tightness of her nipples, that exquisite straining pull. And she was aware of an answering pull between her thighs. An ache. Desperately, she fought against her own traitorous instincts. Desiring Vitor was a pitfall which had to be avoided.

'Then I'd wash away the soap and I'd lick your breasts, suck on your nipples,' he murmured. 'I'd——'

The pyjamas fastened at last, Ashley rose shakily to her feet. 'This isn't. . . I don't. . .you mustn't——' she jabbered.

'I mustn't tell you that I want to bury myself in your body?' he enquired. 'I mustn't say that I want to feel myself deep inside you? Feel you holding me tight? Why not? We both know that the chemistry, or whatever else you want to call it, is still there between us as strong as ever.'

'No,' she said faintly. 'No,' she repeated, her voice firmer this time.

'*Yes*. Why do you think I kissed you when we first met again?' Vitor demanded. 'It was because I couldn't stop myself, because I was driven by the need to know if what I'd felt in Sintra had been real and still existed. It was. It did.' He took a step towards her. 'And now——'

Ashley grabbed up Thomas, using him as a shield.

'He's asleep on his feet,' she yattered. 'I have to put him to bed. Perhaps you could blow out the candles in here and then check that the ones in the living-room are safe? Please,' she implored.

His lips did not move by a fraction of an inch, but the expression in his eyes said he was amused and prepared to bide his time. 'Whatever you wish,' Vitor replied.

As he moved to start dousing the flames, Ashley

fled into the small whitewashed bedroom on the
other side of the hall. She laid Thomas down in his
cot and tucked him up. Crossing to the window, she
stared out at the murky night. The thunder and
lightning seemed to have moved away, but the rain
continued to pour. She closed the curtains. When
was the power going to come back on? Ashley
wondered, as she heard Vitor return to the living-
room. Please let it be soon. If there were electric
light, maybe she would be able to summon up more
resistance against him. If there were electric light,
perhaps she would not feel so agitated, so fevered,
so at risk. She walked back to the cot. Thomas's
eyes had closed and he was already asleep.

'Got any bright ideas about how to stop Vitor
from saying the kind of things he's been saying?'
Ashley asked, speaking softly so that she did not
disturb him. 'If not, I don't know what I'm going to
do.' Disconsolately, she rested her head on the arms
which were folded on the cot rail. 'Yes, I do,' she
said, her head lifting, her body straightening, her
tone suddenly decisive, 'I'm going to tell him that,
while I acknowledge both his lust and mine, I have
absolutely no interest in either. That, whereas I was
once naïve and foolish, I won't be seduced into an
encore. That if he cares so much about persuading
me to quit this house he can have it.'

Ashley frowned down at the little boy. 'I should
also tell him about you. I did try, but it's so difficult.
You see, if I explain to Vitor that he's your father,
anything might happen. *Anything*,' she said, her
tone hushed and anguished. 'It terrifies me and yet I

know I can't keep walking away from it. I know I have to pluck up my courage and tell him that when we made love in Sintra he sired a son. A beautiful little boy.' She bent and kissed his cheek. 'Sleep well, my love.'

It was as Ashley stepped away from the cot that she saw Vitor. He was standing in the half-light in the doorway, watching her. Her throat seized up. She made a hollow sound. Trepidation formed a layer of ice around her heart. There was no need to ask how long he had been there; the intense quality of his stance, his expression, made it plain he had overheard.

'Thomas is my child?' he said.

Ashley nodded helplessly, hopelessly.

There was a long time — several lifetimes — when the only sound was the clatter of the rain against the window, then Vitor walked to the cot. He looked down, and as he gazed at the sleeping child his eyes glittered with what looked suspiciously like unshed tears.

'I was going to — to tell you,' Ashley faltered.

He straightened. His face gave no sign of emotion, though he paused and swallowed before he spoke. 'When? Maybe you were planning to leave it until Thomas reached twenty-one?' he said, his nostrils flaring in contempt.

'No. I wasn't going to leave it for much longer at all. I did attempt to explain the other evening, but —' Her voice cracked, broke, gave out.

Vitor took hold of her elbow in an iron grip. 'We

can't talk here,' he said, and led her out of the room and into the hall.

As he steered her along, resentment stirred. His anger might be justified, but it did not mean she must be treated like a criminal. Experimentally, Ashley tried to pull free, but he refused to release her.

'There was no need to frogmarch me,' she protested, wrenching her arm away when they reached the living-room.

'And there was no need to deceive me.' Vitor closed the door and swung back to her. His face was dark, his fists were clenched, his body quivered with fury. 'How dare you conceal the knowledge that I have a son?' he roared.

Ashley flinched against a question which struck like a lash, yet determinedly stood her ground. Although his wrath frightened her and although she felt guilty, she would not be unnerved, not be fazed, not be pushed around—not when Thomas's future was at stake.

'You didn't believe me when I said I hadn't distracted Simon and you wouldn't have believed me if I'd told you it was your child I might be carrying,' she replied, her voice shaking a little despite all her efforts to project a calm image. Her chin lifted. 'Does that answer your query? With all your business trips, you won't have much time to spare for Thomas,' she carried on, 'and——'

The explosive sound he made stilled her.

'It does not answer it,' Vitor said, his eyes glinting like points of steel in the candlelight. 'While I might have had difficulty believing you at that particular moment two years ago, it was *two years ago*. You've had more than enough time to tell me, and by keeping quiet since we met again you've been effectively lying.'

Ashley looked at him squarely. 'I'm sorry.'

'Sorry?' The word was spat out. 'You deprive me of the start of my son's life, of his babyhood, and you say you're sorry?'

'How was I to know you'd feel like this?' she protested, her guilt sharpening into a defensive anger. 'What happened in Sintra wasn't of any importance to you, so why should the outcome be? All right, my silence was a mistake,' she said hastily, when he frowned, 'but when I told you you might not have accepted that Thomas is yours.'

'Of course he is,' Vitor grated. 'He not only looks like me, he *feels* like mine. I must admit I did wonder, but —' A hand moved, knocking the thought away. 'Are you also sorry for telling Simon it was he who'd made you pregnant?' he demanded, looking at her as though she shed her skin and ate rats whole.

'I didn't,' Ashley said. 'He lied to you. About **that** and about me being his girlfriend. There was nothing sexual between us.'

His lips curled. 'Come on,' he scoffed. 'I saw how familiar the two of you were. I saw that photograph of you both in the paper.'

'The photo wasn't what it seemed. It'd been taken a few years earlier at a family Christmas party when we were playing Musical Chairs. You see, Simon was my foster brother.'

He stared at her through the flickering shadows. 'Foster brother?' he enquired.

'Simon lived with my family from being twelve to seventeen. That's why we were familiar, because we were virtually brother and sister.' Ashley gestured towards the telephone. 'My parents' number is on the pad, so if you don't believe me you can ring them.'

Vitor shook his head. 'That's not necessary.'

'Thomas won't fit easily into your life and he's perfectly content with me,' she said, returning to the subject which was uppermost in her mind. 'OK, you can afford to hire a nanny and you may have contacts with the legal profession here, be on good terms with judges and such. But even though you're endowed with all the wealth, all the push, I'm still——'

'Why did you hide your true relationship with Simon?' he cut in.

Ashley gave an impatient sigh. 'I never wanted to, but he had a chip on his shoulder about people knowing about his past,' she said, and briefly explained.

'I can understand his wish for secrecy,' Vitor said, 'but I don't see the need to adopt the charade that you were his girlfriend.'

'*I* didn't. It was Simon who gave that impression behind my back. As soon as I realised I told him it must stop, but the next thing I knew he was spouting the same fiction to a reporter.'

'The article in Adelaide?' She nodded. 'When

Simon was killed and the media referred to you as his girlfriend, you let it be,' Vitor recalled.

'He'd cared so much about concealing his past when he was alive, it seemed unfair to reveal it after he was dead,' Ashley said ruefully. 'I hadn't expected the papers to pick up on Thomas's birth,' she went on, 'but when they did and when it was taken for granted that he was Simon's I let that be, too.'

'I guess there wasn't much alternative,' Vitor muttered.

'You thought I'd followed Simon to Adelaide,' she continued, 'but I'd gone there on business. I only contacted him because I'd read the article and didn't much like being used.' The lights went on. 'At last!' she exclaimed, and crossed to blow out the candles.

Vitor was frowning, thinking back. 'But when Simon appeared at your hotel you must have talked about us, you told him what had happened in Sintra.' A nerve leapt in his temple. 'How could you do that? He may have been your foster brother, but how could you gossip about something so. . .personal?'

Ashley sat on the sofa. 'There was no gossip. I didn't tell him.'

'Then what the hell made him think you might be pregnant?' he demanded, glaring down at her.

'He said one of the clues was your attitude.'

'My attitude?'

She nodded. According to her foster brother, another clue had been that she had so blatantly considered Vitor to be 'a real cool dude', but she saw no reason to reveal that.

'Simon reckoned that after Sintra if he spoke about me you'd get tense—though you didn't realise he noticed. He said something must have happened and that——' Ashley moistened her lips '—we'd made love. He was guessing, but my face must have given me away.'

'And?' Vitor asked, when she hesitated.

'He remarked on me seeming worried about it and asked if I might be pregnant.' Resolutely, she held his gaze. 'The fear that I could be had begun to haunt my days and keep me awake at nights, and, although I knew Simon was the wrong person to take into my confidence, he was familiar and he was *there*. So I confessed to a possibility, though it was only six weeks since Sintra and there was still room for doubt.'

Sitting down opposite, he digested what she had said.

'So why should Simon tell me that you were three months pregnant by him?' Vitor enquired.

'Because he regarded you as a rival, both on the tracks and off, and by claiming paternity he was claiming he'd made love to me first, before you, and so was claiming the superior position.'

'Simon went to the length of telling all those lies in order to try and thumb his nose at me?' he protested.

Ashley nodded. 'Even though there was a strong risk of him being found out. You see, while his manner towards you may have seemed jovial enough, in reality he was involved in a feud. He regarded you as an opponent whom he was determined to get the better of, in whichever way he could.'

'Why? Granted, we were in competition, but I had no axe to grind with the kid,' Vitor said.

She sighed. 'Simon's childhood had left him with a feeling of inadequacy and a strong envious streak, which meant he found it difficult to live with the idea of an associate being better than him. At school his feuds had taken the form of punch-ups and verbal abuse, but this time — well, if he'd tried to punch you — '

'I'd have flattened him,' Vitor said.

'So he wove a web of lies. But what's important right now is Thomas,' she said, growing impatient of these explanations about her foster brother.

'You're damned right it is,' he growled.

Ashley straightened her spine. 'The best place for him is with me,' she declared. 'You may be prepared to do whatever it takes to get this house, but I'm prepared to do whatever's necessary to ensure that Thomas remains in my care.'

'Your warning is noted, but I don't want to take him away,' Vitor said.

'No?' she said guardedly.

He shook his head. 'Nor would I wish to lock swords with a woman who's become so formidable.' He fingered his jaw. 'That reference to judges; you weren't thinking I might drag you into court and do battle over Thomas?'

She gave a tremulous smile. 'It seemed possible.'

'All I want is for him to be happy and secure,' Vitor assured her, 'which he is with you. I'd never endanger that, I'd never try and separate him from his mother.'

Ashley slumped back against the cushions. 'Thank you,' she said.

'Do your parents know Thomas is mine?' he queried.

'Yes, and so does my brother. But that's all.'

Vitor studied her for a moment. 'Thomas is the reason why you came to Portugal,' he said.

She nodded. 'Even if he only lived here for a few years when he was small, I wanted him to know something of his roots, to be aware of his background.'

'I appreciate that.' Rising to his feet, Vitor stood in front of the fireplace with his legs set apart and his arms folded. 'What we must do now is get married,' he declared.

Ashley stared. Her mouth dropped open. Although she had told Thomas that when she broke the news 'anything' could happen, she had never envisaged this.

'Married?' she echoed.

'You don't want our child to remain illegitimate all his life, to be a bastard?' he demanded.

'Er—no.'

'Neither do I. Nor will I allow Haraldsen to claim him as his.'

'Leif?' Ashley asked, in bewilderment.

Vitor gave a curt nod. 'I may not be able to prevent Thomas becoming his stepson, but I won't agree to him being adopted, nor will he use his name.' His shoulders were thrown back and his jawline became rock-hard. 'It's my blood which flows in Thomas's veins and he'll be legally recognised as mine.'

'But——'

'My son is entitled to his natural heritage and my wealth will be his wealth in time, though as he grows I'll pay for his welfare and his education.' His brow furrowed. 'You will benefit, too.'

In the split-second when he had first mentioned marriage, Ashley had harboured the giddy irrational notion that he might next be going to say he loved her. But it was brutally clear that love was not a feature in his thinking.

'You mean that when we divorce after as short a time as possible you'll give me a lump sum?' she enquired, her voice frigid.

He nodded. 'To be negotiated. I shall be busy for the next couple of weeks,' Vitor continued, gravely making plans, 'but then I'd like us to spend the weekend with my mother so that she can meet her grandson.'

'All right,' she agreed, for the suggestion seemed reasonable.

'I'll pick you up on the Friday afternoon, though I'll be in touch before then,' he said, and bade her a curt farewell.

As he strode towards the door, Ashley regarded him with cold eyes. 'And what date are you thinking of pencilling in for our wedding?' she asked.

'We'll fix that in a fortnight,' Vitor said, stopping to frown. Goodnight.'

CHAPTER SEVEN

DUNGAREES, shorts, T-shirts, socks, sandals, disposable nappies, box of toy cars. A dress, trousers, tops, knickers, bras, nightgown. Ticking off items on a mental list, Ashley decided that everything which might be needed for the weekend had been packed. As she closed the lid of the suitcase and assembled a veritable mountain of carrier bags, she sighed. In an hour's time Vitor would be arriving to collect her and Thomas, but she was full of misgivings. About going to Sintra. About what Margrida d'Arcos's opinion of her might be now that she knew she had indulged in apparently frivolous love with her son. About the idea of marriage.

Ashley walked over to the bedroom window. In his first act as a father, Vitor had arranged for his labourers to build a sandpit at the edge of the terrace and opposite her workshop. Here, as he had been for much of the past week, Thomas was contentedly playing. The little boy's absorption had enabled her to work longer during the days, which meant she had finished the commissions in hand and so could take a weekend off without worrying about them. She slid her hands into the pockets of her shorts. But that still left everything else to worry about.

Leif wanted her, but couldn't care less about Thomas. Vitor was full of concern about Thomas,

yet did not care two hoots about her. She gave a
bleak smile. How ironical. As Ashley gazed out at
the little boy, her chin took on a stubborn slant.
However, she was not prepared to be led by the
nose to the altar. A fortnight ago, she had been too
taken aback by the idea to absorb what it could
imply, but before anything was fixed there were
matters which she and Vitor must discuss, parame-
ters to be defined, agreements which needed to be
cut and dried. A marriage, no matter how brief, was
a complex, problematic business — and her days of
naïveté were over.

All of a sudden, Thomas looked up. He grinned,
clambered to his feet and jiggled excitedly. As she
watched, Vitor strode into view and lifted the child
into his arms. To her annoyance — and her dismay —
Ashley felt her heart break into its usual erratic beat
behind her ribs. In dark trousers and with the sleeves
of a pristine white shirt rolled up to reveal golden,
muscled forearms, Vitor had obviously walked
straight out from behind his desk and into his car.

'You said you'd be here at four,' Ashley protested, going out on to the terrace.

'I managed to get away earlier than expected,' he
replied.

She frowned at Thomas, who had hooked a grimy
arm around his neck.

'He's putting sand all over you.'

'It'll brush off. Besides, a boy's allowed to have a
cuddle when he hasn't seen his daddy, his *papa*, for
a fortnight,' Vitor said, tickling the toddler who

dissolved into giggles. 'Have you decided what you'd like him to call me?'

She nodded. 'I thought that as we're in Portugal——'

'From now on you call me Papá,' Vitor told Thomas. 'Can you say it?'

The child grinned. 'Papá.'

'You call me that because I'm your father,' he said, and shot a glance at Ashley. 'I'm the man who once made love to your mother and made you.'

'Did you manage lunch?' she enquired, ignoring both his look and the remark. Vitor shook his head. 'Would you like a sandwich and a cup of coffee?'

'Please—I could use a break. There's a toy garage for Thomas in the car,' he told her. 'Suppose I give it to him and he can play with it while I eat?'

Ashley nodded, and, as she went off into the kitchen, Vitor took the little boy to collect his present.

'I hope you don't intend to bring him something every time you see him,' she said, returning to the terrace to find the child energetically shunting toy cars in and out of a smartly painted wooden garage. She put the tray she was carrying down on the wrought iron table. 'If so, I——'

'Relax,' Vitor said. 'The last thing I want to do is spoil Thomas or have him look forward to my visits simply because he knows I'll arrive bearing gifts.' He pulled out a chair and sat down. 'I won't. Before I buy him anything in future, I'll confer with you. Scout's honour.'

'Thanks,' she said, and passed him a plate of crusty bread ham and tomato sandwiches.

'I've been thinking about Simon,' he said, as he began to eat, 'and I'd be grateful if you could fill me in on a few things.'

'Such as?' Ashley asked, pouring out two cups of coffee.

'Why he should tell me from day one that you were his girlfriend. Even if he'd already identified me as his deadly rival, at that point it didn't have much relevance.' Vitor looked at her across the table. 'I figure Simon said it because he was in love with you and he hoped that by pretending the two of you were a couple he might give fate a nudge and make it happen.'

Ashley frowned. 'He could have had a bit of a crush,' she acknowledged, 'but the main attraction was my career. Simon liked to impress, and having a girlfriend who was considered to be a high achiever gave him extra kudos. The tragedy is that he didn't need any; he had more than enough kudos of his own from his motor racing,' she said sadly, 'but that's the way he thought.'

'He also had more than a crush,' Vitor declared. 'Ashley, the kid was always so damn *pleased* when you were around. And when he talked about you, which he did a lot, he positively glowed.'

'That was because I came from the most stable period of his life and I made him feel secure.'

'You represented a thumb and a blanket?'

She gave a wry smile. 'Yes.'

'There could have been an element of that, but

Simon was also in love you,' Vitor persisted. 'He told me he'd got in touch again the moment he'd heard that you'd decided to soft pedal a bit on work and so could be open to having a boyfriend.'

'Well, yes, he did,' Ashley acknowledged, frowning.

'Simon reckoned he'd adored you for years and that *he* intended to be that boyfriend, and he'd make it happen by ensuring the two of you were together as much as possible. Apparently he'd fixed up with the travel agency which handled Dalgety's bookings for you to join him at all the Grands Prix.'

'It was a definite arrangement?' she protested.

Vitor nodded. 'The agent was forever calling him, wanting to know if, this time, you'd be taking up the ticket. Though you never did.'

Ashley took a pensive drink of coffee. Because she had been fond of Simon in a sisterly way—as a much older sister—she had always taken it for granted that the affection he had shown her in return had been brotherly, with maybe a spot of heroine worship thrown in. But now, when her mind travelled back, it was clear from the young man's behaviour and some of the comments he had made that she had been suffering from myopia.

'I was wrong,' she said slowly. 'Although it was partly an ego thing, I can see that Simon probably did love me—in his way.'

'I should have realised the two of you weren't a couple,' Vitor reflected, when he had finished his sandwiches. 'When we first met and you spoke about having lunch with Simon, it was one hell of a shock.

You weren't at all what I'd imagined his beloved would be.'

'Which was?'

'The daffy juvenile cheerleader type—but instead you were mature, intelligent, in a very different league.' He grinned crookedly. 'Though you do have cheerleader legs. When you were hanging over that skip the other evening——' he rolled his eyes '—they seemed to go on forever.' He reached for his coffee. 'But if you were wrong about Simon loving you, so I'm wrong about the reason for his accident,' he said, becoming grave.

Ashley looked at him over the rim of her cup. 'Yes?'

Vitor nodded. 'Your comment about him finding it difficult to live with the idea of someone being better than him forced me into a complete rethink. And the more I thought, the more I realised that his *bonhomie* had been superficial. He'd disliked anyone complimenting me and when I'd done well in a race he'd found it difficult to offer congratulations. Adelaide was his last opportunity that season to beat me, so he took a gamble; one which, had he been less driven, he would have known didn't stand a chance of coming off.' His brown eyes darkened. 'I owe you an apology. Simon didn't crash because of you, he crashed because of me.'

She shook her head. 'Simon crashed because of *himself*,' she said firmly.

He was silent for a moment. 'I guess,' he acknowledged.

'And your apology is accepted.'

'Thank you. There have been several times when I was tempted to try and get in touch and apologise for my attack at the time of Simon's death.' Vitor frowned. 'But as I still held the same views it seemed pointless.'

'And there have been several times when I was tempted to try and get in touch and tell you about Thomas,' Ashley said, in a pert rejoinder. Rising, she crossed to the sandpit and lifted out the little boy. 'You have to be washed and changed,' she told him, when he began to noisily protest, 'and then——' she indicated Vitor ' — you can go in your *papá's* motor car.'

The blackmail worked. Thomas's wails subsided and, a quarter of an hour later when they came back out on to the terrace, he was clean, his dark curls had been brushed and he wore a fresh shirt and shorts.

'Aren't you smart?' Vitor said, as the child scampered towards him. His gaze lifted to Ashley. 'Your *múmia* looks like a million dollars, too.'

Her casual clothes had been discarded in favour of a short-sleeved chartreuse-coloured jacket with a matching skirt and high-heeled sandals. It was an outfit from her more prosperous days, and an outfit which was intended to boost her morale. Golden hoops swung from her ears and she wore a fine gold chain around her neck. For the first time in months, her hair had been cut and now swung in a pale honey curtain halfway down her back.

'I'll just take your plate and——' Ashley stopped; the table was empty.

'I've washed and dried everything,' Vitor said. 'I thought it might be diplomatic to take the garage,' he continued, 'so I've cleaned it off and it's in the car.'

She forced a smile. She knew she was being unreasonable, but his domesticity seemed like an intrusion and she resented it.

The house was locked, and Vitor carried her luggage to the car. As he stowed everything in the boot, Ashley noticed dark smudges beneath his eyes. Yet again, he had been overdoing things, she thought tartly.

'Would you like me to drive?' she offered. 'You've already had one long journey today and I'd rather you didn't fall asleep at the wheel.'

'Thanks,' he said, and handed her the keys.

'I know I look tired,' Vitor said, as they set off north, 'and I feel bushed. But since we last met I've visited both the States and Brazil, and had several long days of hard talking.'

Ashley cast him a glance. 'Which seems to be your regular routine,' she said crisply.

'Not any longer. The talking was in order to reorganise the responsibility structure within D'Arcos Limitada,' he told her. 'For the past two years I've made all the decisions, major and minor, though heaven knows why when I employ intelligent, capable, highly qualified managers. However, it's now been arranged that the guys abroad will each run their own particular operation and only call on me when there are policy matters to be discussed.

Which means my overseas trips will be reduced to two or three a year. Which is quite a change.'

'And what happens here in Portugal?' she enquired. 'Will you continue to run the show?'

'Yes, though I shall follow your advice and delegate more. A lot more.' Vitor looked back at Thomas, who was sucking his thumb and growing heavy-eyed. 'I've fixed things so that now I'll have the time to be a hands-on, actively involved father.'

Emotions warred in Ashley's mind. While she wanted the little boy to have the benefit of a strong male influence in his life and grow up rounded, she rebelled against the prospect of Vitor's frequent presence in *hers*. She stared grimly ahead. But she was going to have to keep the door open to him for the next twenty years and, like it or not, it was something that she would have to come to terms with.

'What does Leif think about us getting married?' Vitor enquired some time later as they turned on to an expressway.

'He doesn't think anything,' Ashley replied. 'I haven't told him. I haven't mentioned it to anyone.'

'Why not?'

'Because I'm doubtful about whether we should go ahead.'

Beside her, she felt Vitor stiffen. 'You don't want to legitimise Thomas's position?' he demanded.

Looking through the rear-view mirror, Ashley saw that the little boy had fallen asleep.

'Yes, I do, but——' She hesitated. 'I assume it'd

only be a matter of months before the divorce procedure was set in motion?'

'I guess,' he said, sounding brusque and irritated.

'Even so, before I commit myself to anything I need to know what a marriage would involve.' Ashley cast him a wary glance. 'You aren't intending that we should set up home together? You don't expect us to — to —'

'Indulge in the pleasures of the flesh?' Vitor supplied, when she came to an awkward halt. 'Why not? You were willing enough two years ago.' He placed a hand on her knee. 'And, if I were to use all my available charm, you'd be willing again.'

Ashley's legs were bare, her skirt was short, and the touch of his fingers on her skin aroused a leaping response.

'No!' she squeaked, thinking that, far from it taking all his charm, her willingness could be achieved with only a minimum of persuasion.

'You would,' he murmured, in a voice of maddening certainty, of maddening calm. 'I don't understand why you should get so wound up about the prospect of making love now, when before you were . . .offhand about it.' He began caressing her knee — idly or on purpose? Whichever, Ashley could hardly keep still. 'All right, you became pregnant then, but there is such a thing as birth control and — Watch out!' Vitor yelled, as she swung out to pass a man on an ancient and painfully slow *motorizada* — one of Portugal's ubiquitous two-stroke motorbikes. A coach full of tourists was approaching in the opposite direction, and he let go of her knee to brace both hands protectively against the padded facia. 'Aarghh!' he exclaimed, as the coach shot by.

'I was miles away,' Ashley said.

'Inches. The Portuguese may have the worst road safety record in Europe, but that's no reason to try and add to the casualty figures.'

'We weren't in any danger,' she protested.

Vitor flung her a dubious look. 'How long is it since you last drove a right-hand-drive car on the right side of the road?' he demanded.

'Three or four years.'

'And how long is it since you last drove?'

'About nine months.'

'Now you tell me!'

'I'm perfectly safe, and I'm within the speed-limit,' Ashley added pungently, when he craned forward to inspect the speedometer.

'Only just. You're not overtaking *again*?' he protested, as she drew out beyond a cattle lorry.

'Who's driving this car?' she enquired, with some heat.

'You are.'

'So shut up!'

Vitor sighed. 'Yes, ma'am.'

'Talking about Leif,' Ashley said, when the lorry was safely behind them, 'we won't be joining forces.'

They had not been talking about the Dane, but she felt disinclined to revert to a discussion about the ease with which Vitor could persuade her to go to bed with him.

'The guy would obviously like you to be Senhora Haraldsen,' he said.

'Maybe, but I wouldn't. She looked out at the road ahead. 'I gave you the wrong impression about our relationship. It's purely a business one and it's going to stay that way.'

'So you don't have a man in your life?' Victor said.

'No. I get chatted up from time to time, though if you have a small child——' she glanced through the mirror at Thomas '—not too many men want to become involved. Not seriously. But having affairs doesn't interest me. It never has done. I had a fling with someone when I was at college, but that was the only occasion. Maybe it's unfashionable in these days of shallow and meaningless alliances, but for me love is a serious matter.' Ashley frowned. 'So is marriage. I don't feel comfortable about the prospect of us standing up and swearing oaths which neither of us intends to keep,' she told him. 'It isn't honest. It makes a mockery of the ceremony, a mockery of the whole institution.'

'You're suggesting that our son remains a bastard?' Vitor demanded.

Ashley sighed. She did not really know what she was suggesting.

'Would it be so bad?' she appealed. 'It isn't the stigma that it used to be and——'

'Other people may not care whether Thomas is legitimate or not, but *I* do,' he interjected curtly. He looked at the sleeping child. 'And if he could express an opinion I've no doubt he'd say he cared, too—cared deeply. It may not matter much to you——'

'It does matter,' she protested, 'but——' Aware of

getting nowhere, Ashley changed tack. 'If we should marry——'

'We will,' Vitor stated flatly.

'—and when we divorce, I'm grateful to know you'll pay towards Thomas's upbringing, but I don't want any money for myself.'

'Not even a bona fide payment in thanks for your co-operation and to compensate you for any upheaval?' Vitor enquired, in a sardonic reminder of a phrase he had once used before.

'No, thanks.'

He undid his tie so that it hung loose around his neck and unfastened the top few buttons on his shirt. 'So be it,' he said.

Ashley's fingers curled tighter around the steering-wheel. Limited though it was, his casual masculine undressing disturbed her. She might not be able to see the dark chest hair which curled up towards his throat, but she could imagine it. She frowned. His reference to her 'co-operation' had also disturbed her.

'What are the sleeping arrangements at your mother's?' she enquired, as they drove along.

Vitor slid his hand into the open neck of his shirt and began to rub his chest lazily. 'Sleeping arrangements?'

'You haven't fixed for us to share a room?' Ashley demanded. 'I'm well aware that my silence over Thomas now means you consider me the pits, but it doesn't necessarily mean that you no longer——'

'Lust after your delectable body?' he inserted
She flushed. 'No.'

'We are supposed to be prospective man and wife,' he said, still rubbing his chest, 'and Margrida is under the impression that we're madly in love.'

Ashley turned to gaze at him. 'Madly in love?' she protested.

'Keep your eyes on the road.'

She frowned at the traffic ahead. 'What have you told your mother?' she demanded.

'That we'd had a short but intense affair, and when we'd met again and realised we still felt the same about each other you'd revealed how Thomas was mine.' Vitor leaned forward to open the glove compartment. 'Would you like some chocolate?'

'Er—please.'

He broke a large bar of dark Swiss chocolate into pieces. 'Open up,' he instructed.

Ashley obediently opened her mouth.

'So I'm expected to act as though I'm in love with you?' she enquired, when she had swallowed the chocolate down.

'Margrida will think it strange if you don't. I'm not demanding we spend the entire weekend locked in a clinch,' Vitor said impatiently when she started to protest, 'but we should appear to be on good terms. OK, I can't force you——'

'I can manage the good terms,' Ashley said, 'but I am not, repeat not, sleeping in the same bed! I won't be manoeuvred into a situation where——'

'Open up,' he commanded, and fed her again. 'You're not being manoeuvred into anything. I told my mother that as Thomas would be in strange surroundings and might wake in the night I thought it better if the two of you shared a room. So you'll be with him in the guest room and I'll be in my usual bedroom. How would you feel about overseeing the decoration of the showhouse?' he went on.

'Sorry?' she said, unable to make the necessary mental adjustment.

'When the time comes it'll need to be decorated and furnished to show prospective buyers, and as you've done such a great job on your own place I thought you might be interested,' Vitor explained. 'We'd pay the going rate, and provide a car to enable you to get around to the various stores and liaise with curtain-makers and such.'

Ashley weighed up his suggestion. The assignment would be a challenge which she would enjoy and, if it turned out successfully, maybe interior decorating could become a second string to her tiles? She released a sigh. While all her instincts balked against becoming too enmeshed with Vitor, she seemed destined to fight a losing battle.

'I'd like time to think, but I could be interested,' she told him. 'Will it be the big house which is the showhouse?'

'No, we've decided to leave that for the owners to do up exactly as they wish. The showhouse will be one in the middle price bracket. It has a thirty-five-foot living-room, with — mouth open — ' Vitor ordered, and gave her another piece of chocolate ' — a flight of three steps up to a generously sized dining area. The floor will be tiled in white marble and — '

As they drove on, he described the house in

glowing detail and continued to feed her chocolate. Sometimes his fingers strayed between her lips and when she closed her mouth she accidentally sucked on them. Whenever that happened, a quicksilver feeling went skidding through her bloodstream. How could Vitor tap so effortlessly into her physical awareness—of him, and of her own traitorous desires? Ashley wondered. How was she going to survive this weekend? Her hands gripped the steering-wheel. She would survive by remembering that she was an intelligent capable woman with access to will-power and self-control— and that the two days were not going to last forever.

'No more, thanks,' she said when Vitor offered her another piece of chocolate. 'You trust me to drive without keeping a constant watch?' Ashley enquired pertly when he put away the remains of the bar and rested back his head.

He gave a dry smile. 'I was over-reacting earlier,' he said, and closed his eyes.

Vitor slept for almost an hour and so did Thomas, but both of them awoke as they neared the outskirts of Lisbon, just in time, for now Ashley needed directions, and Vitor navigated them on to a bypass and north along minor roads.

'I'm not happy about us getting married,' Ashley said again, as the hills of Sintra appeared in the distance, 'and I'm——'

'Nearly there,' Vitor said, turning to grin at Thomas.

'You're not listening to me,' she protested.

'I don't need to. Everything you're going to say, you've said before.'

She frowned. 'Even so——'

'Let's get this weekend over and then we'll discuss things in detail,' Vitor cut in impatiently. He pointed ahead. 'You turn in there.'

'Guess what? We arrived all in one piece,' Ashley said, as she drew the car to a halt outside the stone villa.

'We did.' He reached into the glove compartment. 'Unfortunately I'm fresh out of medals to give you, but——'

'No more chocolate, thanks,' she said again, then stared down at the topaz surrounded by a cluster of diamonds which Vitor had slid on to the third finger of her left hand.

'It fits,' he said. 'I hoped it would.'

'Yes, and it's beautiful, but—— What is this?' she protested.

'An engagement ring.'

'Vitor, I can't possibly——'

'It'll keep my mother happy. Here she is,' he said, as the front door of the house opened and Margrida came out to greet them.

Ashley pinned on a smile. It was too late to argue.

'Has Thomas settled happily?' Margrida asked that evening as Ashley returned to the drawing-room.

'He's already asleep,' she reported.

The doting grandmother smiled and chatted about how easily the little boy had accepted her, about how she had been worried he might shy away, but how he had gone straight to her.

'Thomas is such an affectionate child and so like Vitor,' she completed.

'Where is Vitor?' Ashley enquired.

'I've been having problems with the windscreen-washers on my car, so he's in the garage taking a look. This has been one of the happiest days of my life,' Margrida declared, her voice becoming choky, 'and when you and Vitor get married that will be——'

'We haven't fixed a date yet,' she cut in hastily.

'No, but I know my son is impatient to marry his true love and that it won't be long.'

Ashley picked up a magazine from the table. 'True love?' she said, turning a page.

'When my mother left him the topaz, Vitor vowed he would save it until he met his soulmate,' the older woman explained. 'However, although like any attractive red-blooded man he's had his share of romances, apparently he didn't regard any of them as long-term for he never sealed them with the ring.' She smiled. 'But when you came to lunch I knew that *you* would be his soulmate, that the two of you shared an affinity.'

'We hardly spoke to each other,' she protested.

Margrida clicked dismissive fingers. 'Pah! Who needs words? The way you looked at him and how he was continually glancing at you told me it had been love at first sight.' She gave a nostalgic sigh. 'Which is how it was with my husband and me. We met, fell head over heels in love in a shockingly short time, and were still in love thirty years later when he died.' She fell silent, dwelling on her memories, but when the door opened she looked up. 'Ah, Vitor,' Margrida said. 'Have you identified the trouble?'

'Identified it and fixed it.' Walking over to Ashley he bent and dropped a kiss on the top of her head. 'Is our son content?' Vitor enquired.

She kept her eyes fixed on the magazine. 'Our son's fine.'

Later that night, as Thomas slept soundly in a cot beside her, Ashley tossed and turned. The little boy might be content, but she was not. Margrida had been half right, she thought despairingly. For her, it had been love at first sight. She had loved Vitor from their moment of meeting, she was in love with him now and — Ashley thumped at her pillow — she would doubtless still be besotted by the man in another thirty years. Why else had she slept with him so willingly, so precipitately, so foolishly? Admittedly lust was involved, but the major motivation had been that unexplainable, instinctive emotion called love. She had *known* Vitor D'Arcos was her true love and so, with her body, she had plighted her troth. Ashley pummelled at her pillow again. She had experienced the ecstasy, and now she was living through the agony. An agony which could only be intensified if she entered into his very practical, very unfeeling arranged marriage.

CHAPTER EIGHT

ASHLEY clenched her fists, her nails biting into her palms. If Vitor touched her again, she would *scream*. From greeting her with a kiss at breakfast, throughout the morning, and up to ten minutes ago when, at the lunch table, he had covered her hand with his, gazed into her eyes and called her *meu amor*, he had been playing the adoring fiancé to perfection. His mother was entirely hoodwinked and, indeed, had she not known otherwise she would have been hoodwinked herself, Ashley thought despairingly. She frowned down the garden, to where Vitor was kicking a ball to Thomas. Each seemingly fond gesture had wound her up until now she felt as though she were a prisoner in a cell, wondering what her torturer had in mind for her next. Her nails bit harder. They were not due to leave Sintra until early afternoon tomorrow, but she did not think she could stand another day of his kisses and caresses. She did not think she could stand another hour, another minute, another second.

By a fluke, Thomas managed to kick the ball up into the air and her eyes followed Vitor as he leapt to catch it. His bejeaned legs were long and athletic, his body was whipcord-hard. In the sunshine, his burnished head gleamed and the hairs on his arms shone like dark metal. He might have been tired yesterday, but, after a night of what had no doubt been peaceful sleep, he was bursting with vitality and good health. If only he weren't so dauntingly attractive, Ashley thought wistfully. If only he hadn't captured her heart. If only she weren't such a lovesick loon. Frowning, she twisted the topaz ring around her finger. If you want something in this world you have to be positive, she reflected, so, instead of quelling the emotions which arose within her, perhaps she should agree to become Vitor's bride and attempt to capture *his* heart? After all, there was no other woman on the scene and he did desire her.

Ashley gave a curt inner laugh. She was fantasising. The sense of injury Vitor felt over Thomas meant that he also considered her to be devious and untrustworthy, wickedness on two legs. Albeit cheerleader's legs. She tucked her ivory satin shirt tighter into the waistband of her fawn moleskin trousers. Keeping quiet had not only been an error of judgement, it had also poisoned any chance they might have had of entering into a worthwhile relationship.

'That was my friend, Estelle,' Margrida said, coming out from the drawing-room where she had been answering the telephone. 'We'd arranged that she would call in while you and Vitor were here, but unfortunately she's sprained her ankle and is confined to home. Would you mind if we paid her a visit instead?' she appealed. 'I've been introduced to every one of Estelle's six grandchildren and I'd so love for her to see Thomas.'

Ashley's stomach cramped. While she understood Margrida's wish to show off the little boy, visiting her friend would mean extending the deception in which she and Vitor were involved. Mostly Vitor, she amended. But the more people who were actively deceived, the more ill at ease and the more of a villain she would feel.

'If you aren't keen, I could drive Thomas over myself,' the eager grandmother said, sensing her hesitation. 'I'm sure he'd be happy to come with me. It'd give you and Vitor some time alone together,' she added, with a twinkle of her brown eyes.

Down the garden, Vitor had overheard. 'Sounds like a good idea,' he called, and grinned at Ashley. 'Doesn't it?'

She shone a brilliant smile. Margrida's absence would enable her to tell him that she wished him to cut down on the pretending—and on his caresses. Drastically.

'An excellent one,' Ashley agreed.

'Isn't this lovely?' Margrida said to Thomas, a quarter of an hour later when he was in his safety seat in her Renault runabout. She inserted the key into the ignition. 'You're going to see Grandma's best friend.'

Delighted to be taken for another ride in another car, the little boy chuckled.

'I trust Estelle is suitably impressed,' Vitor said, his tone dry.

His mother laughed and switched on the engine. 'She'd better be. I've waited a long time to be able to do this.'

As the Renault set off down the drive, Vitor placed an arm around Ashley's shoulders. 'Estelle's a serious chatterer,' he said, 'so I reckon they'll be gone for at least two hours.'

'Good.'

A smile played on his lips. 'You mean you want to be alone with me as much as I want to be alone with you?' he enquired.

Ashley stood impassive in his embrace, but the minute the car disappeared from view she stepped briskly back.

'What I want is for us to talk long and hard, and *now*,' she declared, and, swivelling on her heel, she marched back into the house.

'I thought we were going to talk after this weekend,' Vitor demurred, strolling after her into the drawing-room.

'There's been a change of plan,' Ashley said sharply. 'Thanks to you.'

'Me?' He raised his brows. 'What have I done?'

'For a start, you've chosen the wrong career, twice. You should have been an actor. But I don't like the way you're pretending to be so fond of me,' she told him, her hazel eyes flashing and her arms akimbo, 'and I don't like the way we're deceiving your mother.' Her voice lowered. 'I *hate* it.'

'Hey,' Vitor murmured, and reached out to put a hand on her shoulder.

Ashley moved away. 'Leave me alone,' she said rawly. 'Don't cash in on the fact that you know I—I'm susceptible to you. You're heartlessly manipulating your mother into believing that we're about to embark on a long and happy marriage, and you're doing it by manipulating me. But, in a very short time, your mother's hopes will be dashed and she'll be upset. And as for me——' To Ashley's dismay, she felt tears well in her eyes. She gave a hasty sniff. The armour of her hostility was essential. The last thing she could afford to do was cry, because if she started she might never stop. 'I know Thomas's legal status is important to you and it is to me,' she said, in a rapid jump of track. 'I'd like him to bear his rightful name, I'd like him to be able to say which family he comes from, I'd like him to hold his head up high in any company—but I won't be bounced into a sham of a marriage, not even for five minutes. I can't. It would crucify me.' She wrenched the ring from her finger and thrust it at him. 'Wearing this crucifies me, too.'

'Hold on,' Vitor protested.

Ashley stopped whatever he had been going to say next with a humourless laugh. 'What is there to hold on to?' she asked. 'Two years ago, our love-making didn't mean anything to you and now this marriage means damn all. Maybe you can glide serenely through, but unfortunately I'm not so——'

'Making love did mean something,' he interjected. For a moment, Vitor gazed at the ring in his hand, then he slid it into his hip pocket. When he raised his eyes, his expression was cool. 'If my memory serves me correct, it was you who declared that it had been of no consequence and to wipe it out,' he said, the adoring fiancé replaced by an aloof accuser.

'Only after you'd told me that you couldn't get

involved. Plain fact,' she said tartly when he seemed about to protest. 'And I was well aware that "couldn't" translated as "wouldn't".'

Vitor studied her for a long, piercing moment. 'So you said to forget about it because of what I——' Dropping down on the sofa, he sank his head into his hands. There was a taut silence. The ormolu clock ticked on the mantelpiece. A bird twittered somewhere. 'I cared about us making love,' he said, raking both hands back through his thick dark hair and looking up at her. 'I cared about you. From us meeting back in the February, I knew you were special. I knew—it sounds corny—but I knew we were meant to be, that we were *simpático*.'

Ashley refused to be beguiled. 'In that case, why give me the no-involvement line?' she demanded.

'Because the Formula One season was in progress.'

'What difference did that make?'

'*All* the difference.'

Her brow furrowed. 'I don't understand. You may have been single-minded about racing, but I was also tied into my work. I didn't have the time, nor would I have expected to be romanced in a way which might have encroached on either of our careers. I knew you were committed and I wasn't going to interrupt.'

'Yes, but——' Vitor sighed. 'Sit down and I'll explain.'

Ashley sat at the other end of the sofa, well away from him. To know he had considered her 'special' was satisfying, but she did not regard it as a signal to fall headlong into his arms. No, siree. She was far too wary and the situation was far more complicated than that.

'For me, being single-minded meant that for the eight months of the racing season every other aspect of my life was put on hold,' Vitor began, 'apart from the construction company. My mother reckoned she had to invite the Dalgety team to lunch every year because it was the only way she could get me to take a day off. She was damn near right, too.' He gave a twisted smile. 'However, Formula One had the priority and I was protective of it. So much so that I deliberately avoided anything outside it which might affect my emotions or disturb my thoughts. For those eight months I wanted a disciplined one-track existence and a focused mind. It was what the Press admired as my dedication, though now it seems more like a selfishness allied to ruthlessness,' he said, frowning.

'How did Celeste fit into all this?' Ashley questioned. 'Didn't she affect your emotions? Didn't she disturb your thoughts from time to time?'

He shook his head in grim negation. 'It sounds lousy, but the great advantage to Celeste — and the reason why our relationship survived for as long as it did — was that she never had much of an impact on either my feelings or my thoughts. We lived together, we slept together, but she didn't intrude. I never allowed her to intrude.'

'Celeste must have realised she wasn't so important to you,' she protested.

'Sure, but she accepted it. After all, I wasn't so

important to her, not on the deep-down emotional level. But you intruded. You, I couldn't stop,' Vitor continued. He gave a wry smile. 'Although it infuriated me, after we first met I was unable to get you out of my mind. I knew you weren't the kind of woman I could conveniently disregard, as I'd disregarded Celeste, and I certainly didn't want to become entangled with my team-mate's girl-friend——'

'Too much emotional hassle, too close to home?'

He nodded. 'But I was forever thinking about you. I tried to tell myself it was purely physical and you were just an object of desire, but I knew it was more than that.'

Ashley looked at him. She could scarcely believe what he was saying.

'Yes?' she said warily.

'Much more,' Vitor vowed. 'When you didn't accept Simon's invitations to the various Grands Prix, I was relieved. Relieved, and yet. . .bereft. Then, when he told me you were coming to Lisboa—— You reckoned Simon was envious. So was I then, of him. So envious it *hurt*.' He was silent for a moment, remembering, then he rallied. 'When I discovered you'd be accompanying him to Margrida's lunch party, I decided that the only way I could handle it was by avoiding you.'

'And you did very successfully, until your mother saddled you with taking me back to my hotel.'

'Which she may have done on purpose.'

Ashley's eyes opened wide. 'You think so? But she believed Simon was my boyfriend.'

'Yes, though afterwards she told me she didn't think he was right for you and she'd never reckoned Celeste was right for me. But she'd taken an instant liking to you and for years she'd been agitating for me to settle down.'

'Yesterday Margrida was saying that when she saw us together at the lunch she felt we shared an affinity,' Ashley recalled.

'Well, whether she indulged in a spot of match-making or not, when we got inside that barn I couldn't keep my hands off you,' Vitor said, and a smile appeared in the corner of his mouth. 'You were desperate for me, too.'

'I was operating by instinct rather than intellect,' she informed him primly.

'Whatever it was, you operated to perfection. Waves crashed and orchestras played.' His expression sobered. 'But afterwards I didn't know what the hell I was going to do about it, about us. At that moment in time I didn't want to become entangled in problems with Simon and Celeste. I didn't want to become entangled with *you*.' Vitor thought again. 'I lie. My heart wanted to be entangled and my body, but not my head. So I decided to put everything on ice for six weeks, until the end of the season.'

Ashley frowned at him along the length of the sofa. 'It never occurred to me that you might be talking about a postponement.'

'I don't suppose it would. Why should it? You knew virtually nothing about me, about the way *I* operated.' There was the glimmer of a smile. 'But thinking I could orchestrate us like that was pretty high-handed.'

'Very high-handed,' she said pungently.

'I should also have recognised I was being unrealistic and I think I did,' Vitor went on. 'Because, although you'd said you understood, I decided I'd better explain, but then had great difficulty in assembling anything which sounded. . .feasible. I'd just about got a speech arranged when you announced that the afternoon had been no big deal!'

Ashley looked beyond his shoulder, out through the French windows to the trees. 'At which point you decided I was a tramp,' she said tonelessly.

'Hell, no!'

She focused on him. 'You didn't?'

'Never,' Vitor said robustly. 'I respected you and I knew you weren't the kind of girl who slept around. If you had been, I wouldn't have come near you.'

Ashley digested this. 'So what did you think when I made my announcement?' she enquired curiously.

'Because I was convinced you'd been as shaken, as moved, by our lovemaking as I, initially it threw me. However, examined in the clear light of another day, I decided you'd felt lousy about cheating on Simon and that dismissing the afternoon had been a get-out.'

'How did you feel about cheating on Celeste?'

'Lousy, too,' Vitor said ruefully, 'though as soon as I kissed you I knew the relationship was over. Despite there being no grand passion, I'd been faithful; but take the faithfulness away and the whole thing crumbled into dust.'

Ashley looked at him. 'So you told Celeste it was the end, regardless of what I'd said?'

'The very next day. I had to because, apart from anything else, I didn't feel I could share a bed with her any longer. After that——' he swore '—if I'd thought about you before we made love, afterwards I thought about you a thousand times more. As time went by, I knew I had to do something, that there was no way I could simply forget you, so I decided that once the final Grand Prix was over I'd get in touch and suggest we meet.'

'With what in mind?'

'A serious liaison.'

'Even though you thought I was fond of Simon, even though you believed I'd felt bad about cheating on him?' she protested.

Vitor nodded. 'I had no difficulty in persuading myself that you'd be willing. And I justified a liaison by telling myself that Simon was far too young to get tied down and that, by taking you off his hands, I'd be doing him a favour,' he said, his tone dry.

'But before you could get in touch Simon and his lies intervened,' Ashley reflected.

'With a vengeance! When he told me you were pregnant by him, it was as though he'd thrown a hand-grenade which blew me apart. I felt so cheated, so broken, devastated. I wished like hell that it could have been my child.'

She gave a sorrowful smile. 'Simon really messed things up.'

'Didn't he just?' he said heavily, and they were both silent for a minute or two, thinking. 'My anger at the time of his death wasn't just because I believed you'd distracted him, it was more complicated than that.' Vitor's brow furrowed. 'Some of it was a lashing back. I wanted to make you suffer the way I was suffering. The way Simon's triumphantly smug statements of impending fatherhood and marriage with you had made me suffer.'

Ashley's eyes went to the thin white scar which snaked from his temple to his jaw. 'And yet you risked your life trying to save him.'

'I had to get the kid out of his car if I could,' he protested.

'If the situation had been reversed, I doubt Simon would have been so generous,' she said ruefully.

Vitor moved his shoulders. 'Maybe not. After that, I realised I'd get nowhere thinking about you,' he continued, 'so I immersed myself in my construction company. I didn't mean to become so intense about it—I had realised my mistake the previous time—but I needed to keep from pining and working a sixteen-hour day seemed to be the only way I could manage it. Though I never managed it in total.'

'Were you still pining when we—we met again?' Ashley enquired haltingly.

He nodded. 'And then, well, although I'd felt that my outburst at the time of Simon's death had wrecked our relationship, I found myself wondering if there was a chance of rekindling it. As soon as I saw you, I knew I hadn't got over you, but I wasn't sure about your feelings.' He grimaced. 'You seemed so eager to get rid of me. But after our day out when we'd had such a good time it seemed as though you might care and that we could have a chance. I decided that once Thomas was in bed I'd tell you I loved you and ask if we could start over, but——'

'But then you discovered how, for two years, I'd been concealing the knowledge of your son from you,' Ashley broke in harshly, 'and telling me went out of the window. Any love you had had for me vanished, even though the sexual attraction remained. I'm not surprised.' As she spoke, the tears which had welled before began to spill from her eyes and down her cheeks. 'I know it's too late now and that it—it doesn't make any difference,' she said raggedly, 'but when I saw you again I knew that I loved you, too. I knew that I'd loved you from the moment we first met and I'd never stopped.'

Vitor moved towards her along the sofa. He seemed fascinated by her tears.

'That's all right, then,' he said.

She took a shuddering breath. 'Sorry?'

'We both love each other. I know this man-woman thing isn't supposed to be easy, but I just wonder how two people who care so much for each other have managed to spend so much time beating each other up,' Vitor said wryly.

Ashley looked at him in bewilderment. 'You mean you can forgive me for not telling you about Thomas?' she asked.

'I have forgiven you. I realise you were desperate to protect him and keep him from harm. I know it was fear which held you back.' He took hold of her hand. 'I'm not surprised. After giving you the brush-off, as you thought, and then bellowing and being so bloody judgemental at the time Simon crashed, I hadn't come over as either sensitive or supportive. You didn't know what I might do and, in the same situation, *I'd* have been fearful.'

She took a handkerchief from her pocket and blew her nose. 'But you've lost fifteen months of Thomas's life,' she said.

'Maybe, yet one thing's for sure—I'm not going to lose you. Not again.' Vitor put his arm around her. 'I haven't been pretending to be in love with you this weekend. I've kept touching you because I still have the greatest difficulty keeping my hands off you, but I was also doing Simon's trick, attempting to nudge fate along. I thought that if I made you realise how strongly I felt you might decide you feel the same.'

A sensation of perfect happiness overwhelmed her.

'And I do,' Ashley assured him.

Vitor drew her closer. '*Eu amo-te*,' he murmured.

'*Eu amo-te*,' she replied, and he kissed her.

His kisses were deep and cherishing and hungry, and it was a long time before they eventually came up for air.

'Will you wear this again?' he asked, stretching back to retrieve the ring from his hip pocket. He looked at her without a smile, and without a frown. 'Will you marry me?'

Ashley grinned. 'When you propose, aren't you supposed to go down on your knees?'

'And beg?' Vitor pressed a theatrical hand to his brow. 'How much can a man stand?' he implored. 'But if my lady insists——'

'I don't,' she said, and laughingly stopped him.

'You will marry me?'

Ashley looked into the dark brown eyes of the man she adored. 'Yes,' she said simply.

'As soon as possible?' Vitor asked, as he slid the topaz ring back on to her finger.

'As soon as it can be arranged.'

He kissed her again.

'I think we should also make love as soon as possible,' he murmured, as his kisses deepened and their breathing began to quicken. 'Like now.' He pulled back to smile. 'And while, in due course, we should provide Thomas with a brother or a sister, on this occasion I suggest we take the appropriate precautions. After all, you do appear to be massively fertile.'

'Or maybe it's you who's massively virile. But precautions are already taken,' Ashley told him. 'You don't think I'd risk getting pregnant by mistake twice?'

He grinned. 'I guess not.'

Drawing her to her feet, he led her up the wide staircase to a comfortable oak-panelled bedroom which overlooked the eucalyptus trees in the garden.

'I thought you were going to undress me very slowly?' she murmured, as his fingers went to the satin-covered buttons on her blouse.

'Did I say that? Right now, I want to rip off all

your clothes with my teeth,' Vitor declared, in a low throaty voice.

Ashley smiled. 'I'd rather you didn't. I'm rather fond of this outfit and it did cost rather a lot of money.

'Spoilsport,' he said, 'but, as you insist, I'll be conventional.'

Coventionality meant that her ivory shirt was deftly stripped off, then her bra. In rapid succession, he unzipped her moleskin trousers and drew the skimpy white lace G-string from her thighs. His dark eyes languorous and heavy-lidded, Vitor looked at her, feasting on her beauty.

'I thought your breasts were delicious before,' he murmured, 'but they're even more enticing now.'

Putting his hands on her shoulders, he drew them slowly down over the full curves, feeling, weighing, drawing a fingertip across the tightening nipples. Ashley shuddered with delight. His hands moved lower across the smoothness of her belly to her hips and he explored the marvels of her body. As a long finger parted the mat of soft fair hair at her thighs, Ashley arched her spine. That wildfire feeling was beginning to grow.

Now she needed to undress him, to feel his skin, to caress his body.

'I'm rather fond of this shirt,' Vitor said, smiling against her mouth as she tugged desperately at the buttons. 'So if I help——'

Soon he was naked. Ashley touched him, stroked him, kissed him. She kissed his nipples and felt the friction of his chest hair against her lips. With a groan, Vitor drew her up against him and pinioned her in his arms. His mouth covered hers in a storm of intemperate kisses and then his head lowered. As she felt the lick of his tongue on her breast, the sharpness of his teeth on their taut points, the wildfire engulfed her entire body. Consumed. Seared. Vitor pulled back, and she noticed that he was trembling as much as she.

'I intended it to last for longer this time, *meu amor*,' he said unevenly, 'much longer, but I'm wild with wanting you and I'm sorry but I can't——'

'I want you, too. Now,' Ashley told him, her voice low and vibrating, and when he slid inside her she was moist and open.

As he pushed solidly into her warmth, she moved, clenching and unclenching her muscles against him.

'Ashley! Oh, God, Ashley!' Vitor muttered, her name hissing out through his teeth in a fevered breath.

The rhythm increased, skin sliding against skin, body moving with body. Their love had no edges, no boundaries. Both gave themselves up to the glory of their passion, until, in a mind-spinning, flooding moment, they became as one.

'Estelle's delight in Thomas made your mother very happy,' Ashley recalled, her head resting against his chest.

'And us fixing a date for our wedding made her very happy, too,' Vitor murmured.

It was midnight, and they were lying together in

his bed. They had just made love again; this time more slowly though just as wonderfully.

'It also pleased my parents and my brother,' she said, remembering the phone calls which had been made.

He lazily caressed her hair, the long pale hair which, earlier, had stroked across his skin and aroused all kinds of tantalising sensations.

'So next on the agenda is deciding where we're going to live.'

Ashley looked up at him. 'I'm happy to move to Lisbon,' she said. 'I like the Algarve, but——'

'Then that's where we'll be. My business is going to be split between the two areas,' Vitor said, 'so either suits me. And if we live on the Algarve it means you can continue with your career. If you want to.'

'I do, for a while. Until we have another baby.' She made a mock bite at his chest. 'Then you'll be in at the start, with the broken nights and the four-hour feeds and the nappies which need to be constantly changed.'

'I can hardly wait,' he said drily, 'but perhaps we could leave it for a couple of years?'

Ashley snuggled closer. 'Let's.'

'What do you think about us moving into the big villa which is being built at Praia do Carvoeiro?' Vitor enquired. 'It should be ready in a couple of months, and we could live in your house until then.'

'And take baths together in the candlelight?'

'Every night,' Vitor said. 'Instead of selling the offices which we've taken over in the village, you

could use them as a workshop and studio,' he
suggested.

Ashley nodded. 'That'd be ideal.' Her mouth
curved. 'You said you'd get me out of my house and
you've managed it.'

'And all it took was marrying you,' he murmured,
and started to kiss her again. 'I shall plant a couple
of almond trees in the garden,' he decided, some
time later. 'Just in case you should get homesick.'

'I won't,' Ashley said. 'Not if you hold me close
in your arms.'

Vitor smiled across the pillow. 'I shall hold you in
them forever, *meu amor*,' he assured her.

THE ALGARVE — 'the playground of Portugal'

Everyone knows that the Algarve is the perfect place for a traditional sea-and-sand holiday, with a wonderful climate and some of the most beautiful beaches in Europe. But it's also one of the great crossroads of the world, where Europe and Africa meet. . .and, because of its turbulent and fascinating history, it's also strongly influenced by the New World and the mysterious East. It's truly a land with something for everyone!

THE ROMANTIC PAST

'Algarve' comes from the Arabic **'Al Gharb'**, the Land of the West, for, like its neighbour Spain, Portugal was ruled for hundreds of years by Moorish princes, who have left their traces in language, cuisine, culture, and above all architecture. But the Algarve was previously occupied by Cyretes,

Phoenicians, Greeks, Carthaginians and Romans, all of whom also left their mark. At **Milreu**, for instance, you can still visit the remains of a noble Roman villa with stunning mosaics.

The Portuguese have always been skilful sailors, and in the fifteenth and sixteenth centuries this expertise led them — under the guidance of the brilliant **Prince Henry the Navigator**, whose heroic statue you can see in the main square of Lagos — on lonely and dangerous voyages to discover new lands. Setting off from the ports of the Algarve, they discovered Brazil, and opened the sea route to India, as well as visiting Africa, North America and Japan. From these and many other lands the explorers — and pirates! — brought back great wealth, as well as exotic spices and foodstuffs that we now take for granted. . .pepper, ginger, paprika, tea, rice — and pineapples!

THE ROMANTIC PRESENT — pastimes for lovers. . .

There's so much more to do in the Algarve than sunbathe! The area has some of the best **sporting facilities** in the world. You'd expect the watersports to be superb, and they are. Whether you choose windsurfing, waterskiing, sailing, fishing or scuba-diving, you'll not be disappointed — but there are also championship-standard golf courses and tennis centres, many of which offer coaching by top professionals. And, if you still have the energy, you can ride, cycle, hike. . .

For the less energetic, the Algarve is dotted with picturesque whitewashed fishing villages which you can explore at your own pace. Many villages have **festivals**, in which they honour their patron saints with religious processions. . .followed by more exuberant secular celebrations of food, wine, traditional music and dancing. You'll be made very welcome, and you may be lucky enough to see — perhaps even to participate in! — the famous regional dance, the *Corridinho*. If you're in the town of Pechão in September you mustn't miss the thousand-year-old *Dança dos Mouros* (dance of the Moors) which recalls far-off battles between Muslims and Christians. The area is much more peaceful and relaxing now!

The whole of Portugal is famous for its distinctive *azulejos* — beautiful decorative tiles, often centuries old, which adorn all kinds of buildings from palaces to railway stations and ordinary houses. Often they're blue and white, showing the influence of oriental pottery, but they can also be seen in stunning yellows and purples, depicting religious scenes, aristocratic figures, or, in more modern times, charming tableaux from everyday life. You won't be able to miss the *azulejos* wherever you go, but in the Algarve the little church of São Laurenço, in Almancil, is especially worth a visit for its outstanding examples of the art form, as well as the beautiful gilded woodcarvings.

By now, you surely deserve a meal—or two! The Algarve has always been famous for its superb **seafood**—delicious fresh, charcoal-grilled **sardines** are a speciality, bearing no resemblance at all to the tinned variety! You should also try **caldo verde**—an unusual green soup—and, of course, **cataplana**, a succulent stew of cockles, smoked pork sausage, ham, tomatoes and onions. But you shouldn't forget dessert, either; the Algarve shows its Arab heritage in mouthwatering confections of eggs, almonds and figs. You may also find a dessert with a name that reflects an interesting history: originating from eighteenth-century monasteries, of all places, there's a delicacy known as *barriga de freiras*. . .nun's belly!

Port and **Madeira** are internationally famous, but while in the Algarve you should take the opportunity to try the less well known but excellent local wine, which has a very high alcohol content. **Vinho Lagoa** is a good example which will, of course, complement the local cuisine. You might also find **Medronho** liqueur, which is distilled from arbutus berries in the town of Monchique.

Portuguese food and wine isn't only excellent—it's also relatively cheap! So you should have some money left for souvenirs. . .and there are plenty to choose from. If you enjoyed *cataplana*, you might want to buy one of the traditional copper vessels in which it's cooked—useful as well as beautiful. You're sure to find plenty of bargains in **knitwear**, and you may not be able to resist painstakingly made

lace, or, especially in Almancil, the local **pottery**. It's made in lovely sunny colours that echo those of the *azulejo* tiles, and it's guaranteed to bring back memories of your holiday in Portugal. You should also look out for hand-woven **baskets** and good quality **leather** bags and shoes.

DID YOU KNOW THAT. . .?

* The Algarve has over **3000** hours of sunshine a year — more than the French Riviera and the Spanish resorts.

* Portugal had a peaceful democratic **revolution** in 1974.

* the famous haunting, romantic Portuguese *fado* music may have originated with homesick fifteenth- and sixteenth-century explorers.

* the Portuguese language still shows enormous **Arab influence**.

* the Portuguese currency is the **escudo**.

* 'I love you' in Portuguese is '*Eu amo-te*'.

POSTCARDS FROM EUROPE

HARLEQUIN
PRESENTS®

Hi!
I can't believe that I'm living on Cyprus—home of Aphrodite, the legendary goddess of love—or that I'm suddenly the owner of a five-star hotel.

Nikolaos Konstantin obviously can't quite believe any of it, either!

Love, Emily

Travel across Europe in 1994 with Harlequin Presents. Collect a new Postcards From Europe title each month!

Don't miss
THE TOUCH OF APHRODITE
by Joanna Mansell
Harlequin Presents #1684

Available in September, wherever Harlequin Presents books are sold.

HPPFE9

MILLION DOLLAR SWEEPSTAKES (III)

No purchase necessary. To enter, follow the directions published. Method of entry may vary. For eligibility, entries must be received no later than March 31, 1996. No liability is assumed for printing errors, lost, late or misdirected entries. Odds of winning are determined by the number of eligible entries distributed and received. Prizewinners will be determined no later than June 30, 1996.

Sweepstakes open to residents of the U.S. (except Puerto Rico), Canada, Europe and Taiwan who are 18 years of age or older. All applicable laws and regulations apply. Sweepstakes offer void wherever prohibited by law. Values of all prizes are in U.S. currency. This sweepstakes is presented by Torstar Corp., its subsidiaries and affiliates, in conjunction with book, merchandise and/or product offerings. For a copy of the Official Rules send a self-addressed, stamped envelope (WA residents need not affix return postage) to: MILLION DOLLAR SWEEPSTAKES (III) Rules, P.O. Box 4573, Blair, NE 68009, USA.

EXTRA BONUS PRIZE DRAWING

No purchase necessary. The Extra Bonus Prize will be awarded in a random drawing to be conducted no later than 5/30/96 from among all entries received. To qualify, entries must be received by 3/31/96 and comply with published directions. Drawing open to residents of the U.S. (except Puerto Rico), Canada, Europe and Taiwan who are 18 years of age or older. All applicable laws and regulations apply; offer void wherever prohibited by law. Odds of winning are dependent upon number of eligibile entries received. Prize is valued in U.S. currency. The offer is presented by Torstar Corp., its subsidiaries and affiliates in conjunction with book, merchandise and/or product offering. For a copy of the Official Rules governing this sweepstakes, send a self-addressed, stamped envelope (WA residents need not affix return postage) to: Extra Bonus Prize Drawing Rules, P.O. Box 4590, Blair, NE 68009, USA.

SWP-H894

HARLEQUIN®
PRESENTS Plus

Nathan Parnell needs a wife and mother for his young son. Sasha Redford and her daughter need a home. It's a match made in heaven, although no one's discussed the small matter of love.

Emily Musgrave and her nephew are on the run. But has she compounded her problems by accepting the help of Sandy McPherson, a total stranger?

Fall in love with Nathan and Sandy—Sasha and Emily do!

Watch for

In Need of a Wife by Emma Darcy
Harlequin Presents Plus #1679

and

Catch Me If You Can by Anne McAllister
Harlequin Presents Plus #1680

Harlequin Presents Plus
The best has just gotten better!

Available in September wherever Harlequin books are sold.

PPLUS16

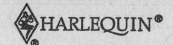

THE WEDDING GAMBLE
Muriel Jensen

Eternity, Massachusetts, was America's wedding town. Paul Bertrand knew this better than anyone—he never should have gotten soused at his friend's rowdy bachelor party. Next morning when he woke up, he found he'd somehow managed to say "I do"—to the woman he'd once jilted! And Christina Bowman had helped launch so many honeymoons, she knew just what to do on theirs!

THE WEDDING GAMBLE, available in September from American Romance, is the fourth book in Harlequin's new cross-line series, **WEDDINGS, INC.**

Be sure to look for the fifth book, **THE VENGEFUL GROOM,** by Sara Wood (Harlequin Presents #1692), coming in October.

WED4

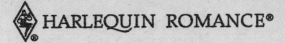

HARLEQUIN ROMANCE®

brings you

KIDS & KISSES

Stories that celebrate love, families and children!

Watch for our next Kids & Kisses title in September.

The Dinosaur Lady
by Anne Marie Duquette
Harlequin Romance #3328

A Romance that will move you and thrill you! By the author of Rescued by Love, On the Line and Neptune's Bride.

Noelle Forrest is "the Dinosaur Lady." Jason Reilly is the eleven-year-old boy who brings her a dinosaur fossil that may be her biggest career break ever—a fossil he found on Matt Caldwell's ranch.

Noelle discovers that there's room in her life and heart for more than just her career. There's room for Jason, who hasn't got a real family of his own—and for Matt, a strong compassionate man who thinks children are more important than dinosaurs....

Available wherever Harlequin books are sold.

Fifty red-blooded, white-hot, true-blue hunks
from every State in the Union!

Look for MEN MADE IN AMERICA! Written by some of
our most popular authors, these stories feature fifty of
the strongest, sexiest men, each from a different state in
the union!

Two titles available every month at your favorite retail
outlet.

In August, look for:

PROS AND CONS by Bethany Campbell
(Massachusetts)
TO TAME A WOLF by Anne McAllister (Michigan)

In September, look for:

WINTER LADY by Janet Joyce (Minnesota)
AFTER THE STORM by Rebecca Flanders (Mississippi)

You won't be able to resist MEN MADE IN AMERICA!

Travel across Europe in 1994
with Harlequin Presents and...

As you travel across Europe in 1994, visiting your favorite countries with your favorite authors, don't forget to collect four proofs of purchase to redeem for an appealing photo album. This photo album can hold over fifty 4" × 6" pictures of your travels and will be a precious keepsake in the years to come!

One proof of purchase can be found in the back pages of each POSTCARDS FROM EUROPE title...one every month until December 1994.